THE
BLOOMSWELL
DIARIES

THE BLOOMSWELL DIARIES

Louis L. Buitendag

Kane Miller
A DIVISION OF EDC PUBLISHING

First Edition 2011
Kane Miller, A Division of EDC Publishing

Text copyright © Louis L. Buitendag, 2011

Illustrations: Adam Ziskie
Jacket design: Kat Godard, DraDog, LLC

For information contact:
Kane Miller, A Division of EDC Publishing
PO Box 470663
Tulsa, OK 74147-0663
www.kanemiller.com
www.edcpub.com

Library of Congress Control Number: 2010933233

Printed in the United States of America
1 2 3 4 5 6 7 8 9 10
ISBN: 978-1-935279-82-2

To my sisters
For always moving mountains for me

Who I am is not important.
Simply allow me to tell you the story…

Chapter 1

AN ORPHAN OF SORTS

Benjamin Sebastian Bloomswell lay in the unfamiliar bed, wide awake, looking at the warm slip of light coming in through the open crack of the bedroom door.

He was listening to his parents repack the last little forgotten bits and pieces from around their bedroom, the tinkle of trinkets sounding as they went back into his mother's vanity case, the tissue paper crinkling softly as clothes were folded and repacked. He listened to the sound of his mother's bracelets as she moved about, the low tones of his father's voice, both of them speaking softly. He knew those sounds very well.

They were the sounds that heralded his parents' departures,

and they woke him up every time. He knew that his parents would soon come into his bedroom to say goodbye. He knew that he would be left with a list of things to do and, more importantly, declarations of their love for him. They had done it countless times before.

But unlike the trips before, this one had the added promise of being the last one for a very long time. It was also different from all the others in that, with his older sister Elizabeth away at her new boarding school in Switzerland, Ben had been brought to stay with his Uncle Lucas in New York City instead of being left back home in England with Olivander and the other servants. He was even allowed to miss school.

Never had Ben been to stay with his uncle by himself for such an extended period of time. In fact, he had never been this far away from home before at all – except for that time when he had accompanied his parents to India. But he had still been a baby then.

The seemingly endless possibilities of what might happen while in America (made somewhat more fanciful by his mother) excited him greatly, but also unsettled him slightly. He simply had no idea what to expect.

Luckily he had always held a deep-seated feeling that he would like his uncle very much. Because the truth was, he hardly knew him. Lucas Bashford had followed a family trend and traveled a great deal because of his job, representing king and country the world over. He was more often than not stationed in far off places for indefinite periods of time, making it seem by contrast as if Ben's parents merely dabbled in foreign travel.

And although this meant that he could always be depended on for exciting tales about exotic locations and daring, if somewhat bizarre, characters, it also meant that to Ben, he was both a stranger and a relative at the same time.

As always, Ben's mother came in first, light from the hallway streaming in after her, playing tricks with her silhouette. She was a tall, slender woman, her long blonde hair pinned up neatly at the back of her head. Ben had quickly shut his eyes and pretended to be asleep the moment he heard her at his door, and he listened as she came towards him. It was their routine. She would sit down next to him and prove she knew he was pretending by making him laugh in some way.

But this time nothing happened. He could sense her standing close to him.

"Faker," was all she said, and he opened his eyes.

She smiled at him and sat down. She regarded him for a moment, and said, "You know I'm going to miss you very much, don't you?"

He nodded.

"And that I love you very much?"

He nodded again.

"And you know that you have to behave yourself and mind your uncle at all times?"

Another nod.

"And you know that I love you very much?"

"You said that one already."

"Oh." She sighed. She thought for a moment. "Well, do you know that I love you very much?"

"Mum!" He smiled. She ran her fingers through his hair and leaned in to give his forehead a kiss.

"I love you, very much," she said quietly.

"I love you, too," he said.

Ben could see that his mother was sad about having to leave him again, and that made him feel a bit better.

"I want to give you something, something I want you to keep safe for me," she said, as she took something out of the folds of her dress.

"What is it?" he asked, sitting up.

His mother opened her hand to reveal a brass key with a small wooden fob attached to it.

"It's the key to No. 4," she said. "It's also a promise."

"A promise?" he asked, taking their London house key from his mother.

"The promise that we won't go home without you."

Ben smiled at this, knowing that his mother meant it. "What about Liza?" he asked.

His mother smiled. "We won't go home without her either. She has the key to Forbes House."

Their country house. "That's okay then," he said, and placed the key on top of his favorite book of stories on the nightstand.

Just then, his father leaned in against the doorway.

"Katherine, the car is here."

"Is it time?" Ben asked.

"Seems like it," she answered. "Ben, you will mind your Uncle Lucas, won't you? He's a busy man. Don't get under his feet. You'll do whatever he says?"

Ben nodded.

His father walked in and put his hand on his wife's shoulder. "We'll see you in time for Christmas, Son. You and Liza," he said.

"And then we can all go home," his mother added.

"Promise me something," Ben said.

"I promise you the moon, my love," she replied, as always.

His parents gave him a hug and a kiss each, his father tucking him back into bed before leaving. When he heard them going down the stairs he got out of bed and slipped out of his room. He stood by the railing and watched his father help his mother with her traveling coat. Barlow, the butler, took the last of the bags out to the car. After his father and uncle shook hands, Katherine Bloomswell embraced her brother tightly, gave him a kiss on the cheek and made for the door. But she happened to glance around and saw Ben standing on the landing.

"You'll see us again soon, my darling," she said, and blew him a kiss.

"See you soon, Son!" said his father, with a wave.

Then they were gone.

Ben heard the car drive off. His uncle waved at them from the doorway, and once they were around the corner and out of sight, he closed the door almost solemnly. He looked up at Ben, his hands in his pockets. He smiled, a bit sheepishly.

"Everything all right? Your room satisfactory?" he eventually asked.

"Yes, thank you," Ben answered.

"Warm enough? I could have Mrs. Pool bring up a hot water bottle, or an extra blanket, perhaps?"

"No, thank you."

"Right."

Another awkward silence. Then, "If you were a bit older I'd offer you a nightcap, but…" he trailed off.

"No, of course not," Ben replied. "Well, I'd best be going back to bed."

"Right you are then," his uncle said.

"Good night, Uncle Lucas."

"Good night, Ben."

Barlow woke Ben up early the next morning by drawing the bedroom curtains. As Ben's eyes adjusted to the morning light, he saw that his clothes had already been laid out for him, next to the pitcher and basin of hot water with which he was expected to wash.

"Good morning, Barlow," said Ben.

Barlow nodded his head and headed for the door. His terse manner unsettled Ben; he acted as if he was annoyed to have to wait on a child.

"Master Bashford awaits you in the conservatory," he said flatly. And with another curt nod, he left the room.

Ben looked around his still unfamiliar room. He felt the uneasy tinge of homesickness lingering somewhere between his chest and his stomach. He reminded himself of his resolution to be brave. There was the excitement of a brand-new city to explore. He gave his neck and face a quick once over with the cloth, got dressed, pocketed the key to No. 4, and ran downstairs to the conservatory, only to find his uncle drinking milky coffee behind an open newspaper.

"Good morning, Uncle Lucas."

For a while there was no response. Then his uncle lazily peered over the top of the newspaper, and it was as if he suddenly recognized Ben. He lowered his newspaper fully.

"Good morning!" he replied, almost making Ben jump. "Sorry! Sorry. Haven't quite gotten used to the fact that there's someone else in this house yet. Sorry. Curse of the bachelor, I guess. When you live alone for too long, you start to think you're the only one around. Especially with the help being as quiet as they are."

"I get like that with Liza when she's back at the end of term," Ben offered. "For the first few days, I keep forgetting she's in the house."

His uncle smiled as he listened, and when he realized that there was no more to Ben's story, he quickly gestured to a chair.

"Do have a seat. Mrs. Pool will be in shortly with your breakfast, I'm sure."

"You're not eating?" Ben asked, as he sat down.

"Oh, I've eaten. Sorry that I couldn't wait; I have to get to the office shortly. Just finishing off some reading before I head out," he said, and he picked up his newspaper again. "Which reminds me…" He placed an extra newspaper in front of Ben. "This is for you."

Ben eyed the fat newspaper with a certain amount of bewilderment. No one had ever just assumed that he read the newspaper, much less bought him one of his very own! He simply didn't know where to begin.

"Is something wrong?" Uncle Lucas asked.

"No, not at all," Ben said. Pulling the newspaper towards himself, he tried to ignore the heavy feeling that suddenly filled his stomach. It was the same feeling he got when he was about to begin a serious amount of homework. "Thank you," he said. He read the headline, and the familiarity of the title struck him. "But this is –"

"*The Evening Standard*, I know!" his uncle confirmed. "I read a British paper every morning. Well, at least, I try to. Why break with tradition? Now don't get too excited, it *is* a few days old." He pointed to the date printed in the corner. "That's the only problem – I have to wait for the shipment to come over. Actually, I've been lucky lately: Up until recently

I used to get a few days' worth in one go – it sometimes took me all weekend just to read them all. Now I'm getting them one at a time." He could see the slight confusion on Ben's face. "You see, it always helps me…with the homesickness and all…having something from home close by, even if it is just a grubby, old newspaper. I thought, you know, maybe it might help you, even if just a bit."

Grubby or not, the newspaper suddenly had a lot more meaning. It was a gift from one homesick person to another. Ben ignored the blazing headline telling of a death in the Royal Family and flipped through the different sections, looking for familiar names and places. He found an article about the British rugby team headlining the sports section. He read a few sentences, but instead of improving his homesickness, it made it worse.

Just then, his uncle stood up and wiped at his mouth with his napkin. "Right, I'm off. The house is yours, explore all you want. Plenty of books in the library. Help yourself."

"Thank you."

"Mrs. Pool has her instructions about tea and such." He made for the doorway, but stopped and turned to Ben. "Perhaps this weekend we can explore some of the city together. Maybe we can take a cab, and, I don't know…"

"That would be nice," Ben replied. He soon heard the front door and his uncle's footsteps on the gravel outside as he walked to the street to hail a cab. Then, as if on cue, Mrs. Pool exploded into the room in a flurry of activity with a tray heaped with silver serving dishes.

"Ah, good morning, Master Ben!" Her cheeks were a bright red, her eyes sparkling and blue under her crisp white bonnet. "Thought I'd forgotten about you, didn't you?" she said, and laughed as if hearing her favorite joke. "Never! Never has a man gone hungry when Mrs. Pool was in the house!"

She placed the tray in front of him and lifted the lid grandly. Two slices of ham, cut thick, lay next to two glistening fried eggs and a mound of crispy fried potatoes that smelled of rosemary and pepper. And on the neighboring plate were four plump pancakes with the pat of butter already halfway melted. Ben's mouth started watering.

"Your uncle insisted I make something nice for your first day here with us. On your own, I mean. Yesterday hardly counts. I barely got to lay eyes on you, much less talk to you! Oh, you do look like your mum, don't you? Handsome as she is pretty!" She was talking a mile a minute! All Ben could do was smile. He couldn't get a word in edgewise.

"I'm sure your sister must be a beauty!" she said, and poured him a cup of hot chocolate. "And your father! Handsome devil, isn't he? Of course, he's no Mr. Pool, but then again, lately neither is Mr. Pool!" She laughed and laughed. "Well, do dig in, my boy. It won't be as good when it's cold," she said, and put the fork into his unresisting hand.

Jack and Katherine Bloomswell had been fully aware of the

danger involved from the beginning. But lives were depending on them.

What they did not expect was such a quick, such a severe and well-planned, retaliation. They were caught off-guard because their priority up to that point, up to leaving Ben in the very capable hands of his uncle, was to ensure the safety of their own children above the safety of anyone or anything else.

All they could do was pray that their preventive measures would hold.

Chapter 2

OLD NEWS IS BAD NEWS

The next morning, Ben did not need anyone to wake him – there was a promise of sightseeing, and he didn't want to waste a single moment. His eyes sprang open when he heard a passing car horn outside, and he was already halfway dressed when there was a knock on his door. Mrs. Pool hardly waited for an answer before she came in, carrying the basin and pitcher on a tray.

"Good morning, Master Ben!" she sang. "Up about already, are you?" She plunked down the tray. "Here, let me give you a hand with that," she said, and set to work knotting Ben's tie.

"I am sorry for being late. Barlow isn't here, and I've

had my hands full seeing to some of his tasks and finishing breakfast. And the good Lord knows," she said, leaning further in as if she was about to reveal a great secret, "I'm not as young as I used to be! There! All perfect."

"Thank you, Mrs. Pool," he said. She gave him a smile and went to the door.

"Oh, Mrs. Pool? Is my uncle in the conservatory?"

"No, love. He slept in on account of it being Saturday and all. I only just woke him. However, I do believe Mary has taken care of the correspondence and left it in the conservatory for him – also something Barlow should have done, but never you mind that. Now, speaking of your uncle, I really do have to see to breakfast."

Ben bounded down the stairs, eager to see if the English rugby team had had any luck, and picked up one of the two newspapers sitting on the breakfast table. He flipped through the pages, briefly scanning each one in search of interesting news.

He saw the name *Bloomswell* first, then *Mr. & Mrs. Jack Bloomswell,* in a small article on the bottom of the fourth page. Seeing their names made him feel as if they were somehow closer than they really were. At least this way he would get current updates on what they were doing, rather than having to wait till they came home and told him and Liza about it all.

But then he saw something amiss, something that seemed odd, in the article about his parents: the words "Bloomswell funeral" and "double burial." He regarded them for a few moments, read a few of the neighboring words, then blinked in case his eyes had lied to him. But no matter how many times he shut and opened his eyes, the poisonous black words refused to change.

He forced himself to read the article from the beginning, conscious of the thickening bile in his throat.

Mr. and Mrs. Jack Bloomswell were laid to rest today after their bodies were discovered side by side late Wednesday evening in the Pendelton Hotel. Authorities are yet to comment on circumstances surrounding the deaths of the prominent husband and wife, but have confirmed that a chief investigator from Scotland Yard has been assigned to the case.

According to the article, which seemed more of a summary of previous articles, the inspector from Scotland Yard had been involved after the police confirmed the couple's disappearance on the fifth of the month, only a few days before their remains were found in the hotel room in the heart of London. The double burial was finally held at Kensal Green Cemetery on Saturday.

Ben was vaguely aware of his uncle greeting one of the maids as he came down the stairs.

"See anything interesting?" he asked jovially, as he entered the conservatory. He peeked over Ben's shoulder to see what he was reading. Ben heard a soft intake of breath as his uncle skimmed the article. Ben turned to face him, his eyes wide.

"Don't worry, everything is fine," his uncle said quickly.

"It says Mum and Dad…Mum and Dad are…" He couldn't allow himself to say the words. As if the universe would hear them and make them true.

"Yes, I know. But –" his uncle tried to explain.

"It says that the police were looking for them for days and that an inspector from Scotland Yard is…"

"I know, but –"

"An inspector from the Yard! That's big!" Ben exclaimed, becoming more and more frantic.

"Yes, but –"

"It says that they had been missing since the fifth. That's… that's… Wait, that's not right!" The facts refused to make sense in his head. He gripped the newspaper, frantically looking to see if he had gotten the dates right. "We were still on the boat on the fifth!" The paper was from last week. He had seen his parents less than forty-eight hours ago!

"Ben!" said Uncle Lucas firmly, as he took hold of Ben's shoulders. "Will you let me explain?"

Questions as loud and fast as steam trains were racing through Ben's head, each of them demanding an answer. But Ben forced out a sigh and allowed his uncle to lead him to the sofa.

"I think we might need a cup of tea for this," he said, and was about to ring for Mrs. Pool when Ben spoke.

"What's going *on*, Uncle Lucas?"

This time it was Uncle Lucas who sighed, as he sat down next to Ben. He looked him straight in the eye.

"Your parents," he started, unsure of where to begin, "did not simply bring you to me while they are away, like some kind of holiday. They did it to ensure your safety."

"My safety? What do you mean?"

"How much do you know about what your parents are doing at the moment?"

"They've gone on a business trip, another business trip. Mum always says she doesn't think what they do is exciting enough to tell me about."

"I'm not so sure that's always the case," Uncle Lucas said, with a snort.

Uncle Lucas was at odds with himself about what to tell his nephew. He knew his sister and brother-in-law had remained vague about exactly what it was they did and for a very specific reason, but things had escalated to a point that none of them had anticipated. Their rule of "the less the children know, the better," seemed to have lost some validity.

"I'm afraid that my sister and your father have yet again managed to get themselves involved in a rather, shall we say, *tricky* situation."

Ben was hanging on his every word. He sensed that this was not the first time his uncle had had to do some explaining for his sister and brother-in-law. Uncle Lucas didn't seem annoyed exactly, it was more a sense of fatigue.

"They've taken it upon themselves to uncover a very

dangerous plot involving some very dangerous people. Now exactly what is going on I'm afraid *I* don't even know, and to be honest, I don't think even your parents know the full extent of what they're involved in. But that is what they have gone to find out. And since they're dealing with the type of people you don't want getting their hands on anything precious to you, especially your children, they've brought you here to me while they see what they can accomplish back in Europe. They've done everything they can to make sure you're safe, and that should explain the rather roundabout way in which they brought you here."

Ben had wondered why they had traveled by boat rather than by something faster, like an airship. Even more puzzling was why they had gone to France before coming here. It would have made more sense to travel directly from London rather than going via Bourgogne. He now realized it wasn't unintentional at all, but a way for them to lose anyone who might have been following them.

"Why 'especially your children'?"

"If those people got to you, used you as a bartering tool, who knows what they could make Mum and Dad do to ensure your safety."

A thought struck Ben.

"But what about Liza?"

"Well, it was decided that Liza would be in safe hands at St. Catharine's, and that the two of you would be best taken care of separately. You're each less likely to be identified without the other, minimizing your chances of discovery."

"But what about this, then?" Ben asked, holding up the newspaper.

"That's where I'm a little confused as well. I mean, there was a time, before you were born, when it was odd for your parents *not* to be in the newspaper. But this, well, it's not something your parents talked to me about. I am not sure if it is one of their ruses or not."

"Ruses? You mean they might be pretending to be dead as a trick?" This shocked Ben immensely. "Why would they do that?"

"Well, considering the people that they're dealing with, it could be a way for your parents to make people believe that they're no longer a threat to them, that they're out of the picture. After all, a dead man can't really do much to get in your way, can he? If you think about it, it's a bit clever. A bit elaborate, I'll say, but clever."

"So they're not dead after all?" Ben wanted to confirm.

"Certainly not," Uncle Lucas answered, almost indignantly. But Ben could tell that his uncle was concerned.

"So, they're fine? Everything's all right?"

Uncle Lucas didn't answer.

"So they are *fine*, right?" Ben pressed.

Uncle Lucas's answer was blunt and almost devoid of feeling. "For now. But if they didn't plant that article then I'm afraid the stakes have been raised, and they're in greater danger than we all thought."

"Why?"

"If the article is real then it means two people are dead as a result of your parents' involvement. And for them to be named so publicly like that, it also means that The Buyer now knows who your mother and father are."

"Who's The Buyer?"

As soon as he asked that question, his uncle looked like he had seen a ghost. A few moments later, when he had still not answered him, Ben asked again.

"Who's The Buyer, Uncle Lucas?"

"Oh, dear," he said, squeezing his eyes shut.

"What's wrong?"

"Katherine is going to murder me."

"Why? What's the matter?"

"I'm afraid your uncle is a bit of a baboon, my boy," Uncle Lucas said, rubbing his hand over his face in annoyance. "He's let a rather big cat out of the bag."

"How?"

"No good can come of you knowing that name," he said, with a sigh.

"Who is he?"

Uncle Lucas looked at Ben and knew he wouldn't be allowed *not* to give him any answers. He had dug the hole he was in, and he would have to find a way out of it again.

"Ben, The Buyer is the man that your mum and dad have gone to find. They think he's the man who is behind whatever it is that's going on."

"Why is that such a bad thing?"

"Well, The Buyer is a dangerous man in that he employs a lot of very bad people, people who will stop at nothing to get him what he wants. Once The Buyer has his mind made up to do or get something, he seems to be unstoppable. Authorities have linked him to many crimes all over the world; they're just never sure in what capacity he's been involved. And until your mum found out, nobody knew who he really was."

"Mum found out who he was? How?"

"She never told me."

"But, even if The Buyer was responsible for the article, doesn't that mean he now *does* think that Mum and Dad are dead? Thinks he's had them killed? So, even if it wasn't Mum and Dad's trick, it helps them anyway, doesn't it? People will think they're no longer a threat?"

"No. If The Buyer meant to dispose of them he would make very sure of things. There would be no case of mistaken identities on his part. Unless, of course, he was up to something."

"Like what?"

"He could be sending them a warning. They know who he is, and he could be telling them he knows who they are, too. Perhaps it's his way of telling them to back off, or else suffer the fate he obviously has planned for them."

"So what happens now? What do we do? What do I do?"

"Nothing, perhaps."

"Nothing?" Ben asked, shocked.

"Now hear me out. If your parents *did* plant the article, then our involvement might undermine what their plans are. If we start sticking our noses in where they don't belong, we might blow their cover and put them in more danger."

"And if they *didn't* plant the article?"

Uncle Lucas thought about this for a moment.

"Then they need to know what's going on so that they can prepare appropriately. Which means we call in some favors, try to find out what is going on and make sure they know what's happening. I can send a wire, intercept them somewhere."

"What about Olivander? Olivander can help, surely?"

"He already is helping, my boy."

"Oh."

"It probably is a lot to take in all at once, isn't it?"

Ben nodded his head. He was more concerned with the well-being of his parents than the details of things.

"Is there anything else you want to ask?"

Ben could not think of a single thing to ask his uncle. He just wished that Liza were there, too.

"Did they know they might get into trouble?" Ben asked eventually.

"They did. That's why they wanted to make sure you and Liza would be safe."

"But if they knew, then why'd they do it? I mean, why take the chance?"

Lucas knew that he had to be very careful in answering

this particular question. "Sometimes, my boy, doing the right thing is the only option. Your mum and dad knew that what was going on was a lot bigger than just their family, and they couldn't simply sit by as other people continued to get hurt. They knew that they could do something to help, and so they set about it, knowing the possible consequences."

Ben was torn between feeling very proud of his own mum and dad and being angry with them for risking everything, simply to help some random people he had never met.

When Ben didn't ask any more questions, Uncle Lucas asked him whether he would like a cup of tea.

"It might make you feel better, even if just a bit."

"No, thank you." Ben glanced back down at the newspaper in his lap, the names of his parents making his stomach turn.

"I'll go make some calls," Uncle Lucas said, and he went into his study, shutting the door behind him.

Ben was left alone in the conservatory, suddenly aware of how awfully far away from home he was. And without thinking, he took the key to No. 4 out of his pocket.

Chapter 3

SIBLING-A-RING-RING

"Ben, I can't seem to get anyone helpful on the phone from here. Everything's closed because of the weekend, so I need to go into the office to see what can be done," Uncle Lucas said, when he finally came out of his study.

"Barlow?" he called, and then remembered his butler had not shown up to work that day. "Blast, where is that man? Mrs. Pool? Mary?" he called, as he went to the front door for his coat and walking stick. Both Mary and Mrs. Pool came around the corner as he reached for his hat. Mrs. Pool stepped forward and helped him with his coat.

"Mary, a taxicab, please," he said.

"Mrs. Pool, I am going to the office on some unexpected

business. Do see to Master Ben here, would you?"

"Of course, sir," she said, and placed her arm across Ben's shoulders, her usual cheeriness replaced by an air of efficiency.

"I'd like to come with you," Ben said.

"I know you would, but under the circumstances I'd rather you stay here – by the telephone, in case someone calls. I've left some messages for people to ring me back. In the meantime, Mrs. Pool here, and Mary, of course, will keep you company until I return. I'll be back as soon as I can. Mrs. Pool, Ben's not had anything to eat yet."

"I'm not hungry," Ben said.

"I can understand why you might not be, but don't go starving yourself. That won't do anyone any good. Understand?"

Ben nodded.

"I don't expect to be home for tea, Mrs. Pool. Please don't wait for me."

"Yes, sir."

He gripped Ben's shoulder, looking him straight in the eyes. "Everything is going to be fine, Ben. Okay?"

Really wanting to believe those words, Ben nodded again.

Ben read the article what seemed like a hundred times that afternoon, trying to make sense of everything. He was grateful for the fact that, even though it wasn't the truth, at least all his parents' article reported was that they had gone missing and then were found dead. They hadn't been burned, staked, drowned or anything horrible like that.

He looked at the date on top of the page again and tried to work out how it was possible that the dates could have been mixed up.

Then he had an idea.

He ran down to Mrs. Pool in the kitchen and asked her where the old newspapers were kept. He was going to see if he could piece together his parents' story, hopefully all the way back to the day they went missing. If by chance it was the same day that they had boarded the ship, it would make sense! But Mrs. Pool did not have good news.

"Oh, Master Ben, I'm afraid we use those to help light the fires, love. There aren't that many left. I'll certainly give you what we have, but I'm afraid it'll only be a couple of days' worth."

Ben took what she could give him and scoured the papers for any news of his parents. He even looked for any mention of The Buyer, but he came up empty on both counts. The newspapers didn't go back far enough.

And since a funeral was a pretty definite ending to a story, he couldn't assume that tomorrow's newspaper would have a follow-up article, but he hoped that it would – anything that might tell him more of what was going on. There were so many questions, but there was no one around to ask! Mrs. Pool was of no help, other than making endless cups of tea, which seemed to be her solution for everything.

Ben wondered if Liza had been let in on their parents' plan prior to leaving for school, or if she was as unsuspecting as he had been. And did she know of the turn of events? If not, could she by chance also discover what was going on? He wondered if the Swiss newspapers would carry a story about their parents, too. And if they were to report on it, would Liza be able to see it? Did St. Catharine's get the newspapers?

Ben took to pacing the floor, walking up and down the hallway between the conservatory and his uncle's study, staying close to the telephone in case anyone called. So far, there had been no word from his uncle. Worry about how he would explain the situation to Liza mixed with the nauseating concern that he might never see his parents again.

You'll see us again soon, my darling, he remembered his mother saying. But that was before their obituaries appeared in a week-old newspaper.

Throughout the afternoon he was constantly overcome by glimpses of a future in which his parents were not there. What would happen to Liza and him? Would they be allowed to stay in their home? And who would take care of them? Uncle Lucas? Olivander? He had heard horror stories of orphaned children before. The work house, the streets. Absolutely nothing like the life they were accustomed to. *They would be orphans.*

His heart nearly stopped when the phone rang late in the afternoon. It could only mean news from his uncle! He sprinted to the study, plucked the receiver from its cradle and pushed it against his ear.

"Hello? Hello!"

The static on the line was incredible; there was nothing but a haphazard scratching and whistling.

"Hello? Uncle Lucas?" He listened intently. "Hello?"

"*Whirr*-Lucas!" shouted the voice on the other end. "Lou-*sizzle-sizzle*-abeth-*sizzle-crack-sizzle*!" Even as bad as the line was, Ben thought he recognized his sister's voice.

"Lizzie?"

"*Sizzle-sizzle-whirrsizzlewhirr*-cas, can *sizzle* hear me? *Sizzle whirr snap crack*!"

"Lizzie! It's Ben!" he shouted, all of his fear and anxiety gone, if only for a brief moment. What would he tell her? Where would he begin?

"*Zwirr*-ucas? I need to speak to Mr. Bash-*sizzle* urgent-*zwirr* Saint Cath-*wirr* compromised *snap* I'm in troub-*zwirr* *zwirr-rate* dang-*zwirr*!"

"Liza! It's me, Ben! I can't hear you! Liza?" Ben shouted into the receiver.

"Get-*sizzle-sizzle* Saint Catharine's! Something's wron-*zowee*! I'm scared for-*sizzle-crack-sizzle*!"

And then suddenly, the line cleared, and he heard, "Tell Mr. Bashford his niece is in danger!" And then the line went dead.

"Lizzie! Liza?" shouted Ben.

But there was nothing, not even static. "Liza?"

He reluctantly set the receiver down. He had held it to his ear so hard that it had pressed a red ring into his skin. His head was now trying to do two things at once – stop spinning and work out a plan. But as he registered what his sister had said, her words suddenly brought all his terrible confusion to a screeching halt: Liza was in trouble, and she needed help.

With a sudden surge of determination, he took the receiver from its cradle again and was about to ring for the operator for a connection when he realized he didn't know Uncle Lucas's work details. He looked around the office for something like a letter or an address book which might help, then thought Mrs. Pool would know his uncle's number. He ran to ask her.

"It's Saturday, love," she explained, as she wrote the number down for him. "You'll be hard pressed to get anyone to answer the phone over there. But here you are," she said. "There's no harm in trying."

Back in his uncle's study, Ben waited with baited breath as the operator tried the connection. Her silence seemed to go on for an eternity, and when she finally did speak again, she did not have good news.

"There doesn't seem to be an operator on duty there to receive the call."

"Would you mind terribly trying again, please? It is very important," Ben said.

"Hold please," she said, with a sigh. "No, there's no one

there. Do you have another connection?"

"No. No, thank you," he said, and again put the receiver down.

There was nothing he could do except wait for his uncle to either return home, or to call him from wherever he was.

Later that night, after the agonizingly slow day, Ben sat on the main staircase waiting for his uncle to return. Uncle Lucas had missed both tea and supper, and he had still not let them know what was going on.

Ben gazed around the entryway to his uncle's house, suddenly aware of how much it reminded him of his own home and the marvelous parties his parents had thrown in both No. 4 and Forbes House. He particularly liked the way the chandeliers shimmered in the gaslight and candlelight, lazily throwing their shadows against the walls. He shut his eyes and tried to imagine that he was back in No. 4, that he was back home with everything he knew – and most importantly, that his parents were but a room or so away.

Mrs. Pool had gone to the trouble of igniting every available light in the house. She said nothing chased the blue devils away better than a little more light on things.

"Master Ben, I'm afraid it's past your bedtime," said Mrs. Pool, who had snuck up on him. "Mary's gone ahead and drawn the covers for you. You can have your bath in the morning."

Mrs. Pool could see that Ben had become seriously

disheartened. "Just think," she said, "when you wake up in the morning, your uncle will be back, and he can answer all of your questions."

"Won't you wake me when he returns tonight?"

"I'll ask him what he thinks, I promise. Best get going, then. Wouldn't want to get old Missus Pool into trouble, would we?" she said kindly.

Ben smiled at her as best he could, then bade her a good night before dragging himself up to his bedroom and away from the front door.

Ben had fallen asleep, still with his day clothes on, on top of the bed, but his sleep was wracked with nightmares, and he woke up frequently. Finally, wondering what time it was and whether or not Uncle Lucas had returned home yet, he ventured from his bedroom to have a look. Mrs. Pool had since extinguished almost all of the lights, leaving just a chosen few lit for his uncle to see by when he returned – a clear indication that he had not done so yet.

Ben trudged back to his bedroom, shut the door behind him, and curled up on his bed. From outside he could hear the footfalls of a lone horse and carriage on the cobbled streets.

Suddenly, he could hear movement inside the house. Someone was coming up the stairs, trying to be as quiet as possible. He sat bolt upright in bed and looked at the door.

Was his uncle finally home with urgent news he simply had to relay? His bedroom door opened quickly. Even in the dark he could recognize the squat figure of Mrs. Pool. She had on her traveling cloak and a hat. The stairs had winded her, but that didn't stop her.

"Master Ben? Master Ben!" she insisted in a whisper. "My love, you have to come with me right away! Oh, good, you're dressed."

"Mrs. Pool? What's the matter?" he asked, as he swung his legs off the bed.

"I can't explain now, love," she said, as she threw his coat down onto the bed next to him. She grabbed his boots from the floor. "Put these on, love. We have to hurry."

He realized her heavy breathing wasn't just from hurrying. Something was making her very nervous.

"Is it my uncle?"

"He told me to come, yes."

"Is he okay? Has something happened to him?"

Mrs. Pool did not answer.

"Mrs. Pool! Is he okay?"

"I don't know, sir," she said, "but we have to get you out of this house!"

Mrs. Pool took hold of his hand and quickly led him down the stairs into the main hallway. Outside, the wind had started blowing. Ben could hear it howl as it curled itself around the corners of the house.

"Wait here," she said. She ran down to the kitchen,

lighting a candle for the first time as she went into the pantry. From one of the top shelves she brought down a small jar of Lyon's Golden Syrup which she pried open with the back of a spoon. Inside was a roll of money, held together by a piece of twine.

She ran back to Ben, and they heard the sound of a car pulling up on the cobbled driveway outside.

Ben's heart fired in his chest – Uncle Lucas had finally come home! He flung open the front door just as an unfamiliar car came to a stop. It was followed by a police truck. He recognized Barlow, who got out from behind the steering wheel of the car and opened the rear door. More than one passenger got out.

In the dark, it was difficult to see which one of the shadowy figures his uncle was. But before Ben could get close enough to see, he collided with another man who had suddenly appeared out of the shadows at the side of the gate. There was a loud gong sound as Ben fell over backwards. The man however, remained standing, completely unshaken. When Ben looked up, he saw that it wasn't a man of flesh and blood, but one of cold, smooth metal. He was staring at a tinman!

Ben scrambled backwards like a startled crab, the tinman moving quickly to stay close to him, until he reached the bottom of the steps.

"Benjamin Bloomswell?" asked a heavyset man, who had come towards him from the car.

Ben looked up at him and saw a flash of white where his

right eye was supposed to be.

"Yes?" he said uncertainly.

"I'm afraid I'm the bearer of some very bad news."

Chapter 4

SUGAR MAKES SWEET

Ben was offered no explanation as to exactly how his uncle had died. He was only told that while his death had been accidental, it had also been quite messy and violent. The policeman relaying the news relished that particular detail a little too much, in Ben's opinion. He was also told that, since he was now apparently guardian-less, he was to accompany the men who claimed to be from the Juvenile Protection Agency. Ben did not believe them and proved his disbelief by trying to run back into the house. Under orders, the tinman pursued.

Ben had only ever seen tinmen from afar and then only in England. He had secretly been impressed by them, by their austere presence and abilities. But because his father had always refused to take even a domestic model into his employ – had so mistrusted them – Ben had also been wary of them.

American tinmen, the so-called "second generation," were different from the original British ones. They were hardly ever seen with the visible *familia insignias* that imbued them with their loyalties. They were streamlined and sleeker than their English counterparts. And in Ben's very limited experience, they were also a lot meaner.

This tinman, with its eerily docile face, effortlessly chased him into the house and tackled him before he could reach the stairs, slamming Ben's body onto the floor with its own, its arms around Ben's waist in a vise-like grip. Ben looked up at Barlow for help, but Barlow did nothing. He just watched.

That's when Ben shouted. "Mrs. Pool!"

Mrs. Pool emerged from the shadows behind the policeman who had followed the tinman. The man didn't have time to react before the iron frying pan connected with his head, dropping him like a sack of potatoes. But in the brief moment Mrs. Pool took to make sure he would no longer be a threat, Barlow was on top of her. He wrestled the frying pan from her hand, clamped his hand over her mouth and dragged her back into the dark recesses of the house. Ben stared helplessly.

Barlow soon returned, alone and unscathed. With one deft movement, Ben was yanked from underneath the tinman and a rag was stuffed into his mouth. The tinman remained on the floor, but turned over onto its back, lying there, waiting. Ben's efforts to free himself from Barlow's grip lessened as he watched the tinman's torso opened like the lid of a suitcase, revealing a fine and intricate network of copper gears, springs and cogs. There was movement everywhere, like ants on an anthill. They weren't actually planning to put him *in there*, were they? Ben redoubled his efforts to free himself. With one quick jerk of his head he managed to twist his mouth just enough to sink his teeth in between Barlow's thumb and forefinger. Barlow screamed in pain and jerked his hand away, giving Ben enough time to spit the rag out and yell for help. Barlow tightened his grip and lifted his free hand to strike Ben. He stopped when the heavyset man spoke.

"This is taking an awfully long time," he said, watching from the shadows, his white eye glinting whenever it caught the light.

Barlow glowered at Ben and clamped his hand back over Ben's mouth, forcing it shut. The policeman, recovered from Mrs. Pool's attack, fumbled to get a bottle from his trouser pocket, saying, "A little chloroform should take care of him."

He tipped the contents of the bottle onto the rag and quickly swapped it for Barlow's hand, pressing it over Ben's mouth and nose. Ben sagged, hanging like a rag from a clothespin, and was flopped into the tinman.

"Remember the hair," said the heavyset man.

A pair of clippers was produced, and Ben's hair was cut off in quick, uneven strokes. Then, after some careful rearranging, they welded the torso of the tinman shut.

When Ben finally regained consciousness, he was soaked with sweat; the inside of the metal body was like an oven. He could almost taste the sour, faintly sweet smell of the tinman in the back of his throat, the only fresh air coming from its cut-out eye sockets. His entire body seemed to hurt all at once. His chest was sore, his head pounded as if he had been punched, and it felt as if he had been pinched quite hard on various parts of his body. With his head inside the head of the tinman, his chin rested on the inside of the tinman's chin, causing the rest of his body to half-sit, half-dangle uncomfortably from his neck – the tinman's body was much bigger than his own.

Ben tried to move his arms and legs, but he could not make them budge. He tilted his head forward to look through the eye sockets, and when he could not make out where he was, he yelled to get attention. Or he tried to. They had stuffed the rag back into his mouth and secured it with a piece of tape. His yell was nothing more than a moan.

He became aware of the rush of tires on the road and realized that he was in the back of the truck. He wondered what was in store for him, but he was also angry, and worried about Liza.

Maybe all was not lost just yet! Maybe Uncle Lucas could… Uncle Lucas could…then he remembered what the man had said about his uncle, and his mind went all sick with sorrow.

Ben drifted in and out of sleep. The trip was long. It seemed much later when he finally heard the sounds of the truck as it drove off the even surface of the main road and onto the uneven gravel of a driveway, eventually coming to a dusty stop, stones shooting out from underneath the tires.

"Hey! Wake up!" he heard Barlow shouting. The policeman groaned his disapproval.

"Wake up!" Barlow ordered again, and Ben heard a sharp smack.

"Ow! My head!"

"Well, then, wake up! We're here."

"Where?"

"Sugarhill."

"What? Already? You could have warned me, you know!"

The truck doors slammed shut, and Ben heard footsteps outside on the gravel.

"Open the truck, we're already late," Barlow said. Weak morning sunlight spilled into the back of the truck as the doors opened.

The tinman did everything it was told, standing up and getting out of the truck while Ben's own arms and legs jerked around helplessly inside of it. Ben realized why he'd felt like he'd been pinched – the slightest movement of the tinman set off a string of counter movements inside it, the small mechanisms eagerly grabbing hold of any of Ben's skin that was too close. Ben quickly tried to work out what position would keep him the safest, and found that by pressing down into the tinman's arms, he could manage to keep somewhat clear of the moving parts.

When the tinman finally stood still again, Ben tilted his head forward to bring his eyes closer to its eyeholes and peered out. What he saw filled him with dread.

The Sugarhill School for Boys, the sign said. It stood in front of the large, mold-colored building almost hidden by trees. Many of its windows were boarded up from the outside with sheets of wood, and weeds flourished unhindered all around. A wiry wisp of smoke trailed out of one of the chimneys, and Ben could hear crows cawing in the distance. It was exactly what a haunted house would look like.

Barlow stepped out in front of him and stared at the building as well. "Sugarhill, huh? Nothing sweet about this place. Come on." He motioned to the policeman and the tinman and led the way up to the front door. Ben didn't right himself in time, and as the tinman stepped forward again, Ben's inner thigh was pinched in the tinman's leg gear. Ben whimpered in pain, unable to sooth the growing welt by rubbing it. He felt like screaming, tears welling in his eyes. He bit into the rag and waited for the pain to subside.

Barlow was about to knock on the door when he turned around and noticed that the policeman had remained back by the truck.

"Cletus!" he barked.

"Why do I have to go in? The kid's already in the suit!"

Barlow eyed Cletus from on top of the landing. Then he slowly tilted his head to the left, and after a few more seconds, jerked his body forward as if he was about to jump down the steps. Cletus sprang into action.

"All right! All right! I'm coming." Cletus hurried towards them.

Barlow knocked on the door and waited.

"Let's do this quickly, yeah? This place gives me the creeps," Cletus said. "I've heard what happens to the kids here. The dogs. The experiments."

"Why are you whispering?"

Cletus's eyes darted around. "This place would give anyone nightmares."

Barlow smirked.

"Don't act like you don't care! I saw how you looked at the place."

Barlow glared at Cletus. He knocked on the door again.

"Why do you think they called it Sugarhill anyway?" Cletus asked.

"Sugar makes things sweet, doesn't it?"

"Yeah?"

"Boys need manners, don't they?"

"Yeah?"

"Sugarhill's where they get them."

After what seemed like an eternity, they heard the door being unlocked from the inside. From the sound of it, there were multiple locks, each one more demanding than the first. Eventually, the heavy wooden door opened a crack, and a pair of tired, puffy eyes stared at them from within. When no enquiry was made as to what they wanted, Barlow cleared his throat.

"We've got the boy Mr. Purchase called about," he said. "You'll want to let him in."

The old man slowly looked to the left and then to the right of Barlow and Cletus, then looked straight at Barlow with a raised eyebrow.

"He's inside here," Barlow said, jerking his thumb towards the tinman.

There was a slight pause as the man regarded the tinman, and the door opened further. They stared down into the dark hallway, Ben straining to see. Cletus swallowed loudly.

Barlow suddenly banged on the tinman's back. "There you go," he whispered at Ben. "Welcome home." Then he instructed the tinman to enter the house.

"He wants to see all of you," said the old man, from inside the house.

Cletus looked over to Barlow for help, but Barlow didn't seem at ease either.

"All of us?" he asked.

"All of you."

They stepped over the threshold.

Chapter 5

THE OTHER MR. PURCHASE

Ben was instantly hit by the smell of the place. It was a stale and musky smell, like old leather shoes and perfume – the flowery kind Ben's great-grandmother used to wear. Behind him, he could hear the slow, methodical ticking of a grandfather clock. Aside from that, the place was eerily quiet.

The three of them were led through dimly lit hallways and corridors, then finally up a rickety staircase that creaked under their weight. Ben imagined that every one of the tinman's footsteps brought up a little cloud of dust around its feet. When they got upstairs, the air around them was thick and fusty.

"Wait here," instructed the old man, when they'd stopped in front of a closed door at the end of another short hallway. The old man knocked, waited a few seconds and then slipped through the door without receiving an answer. A moment later there was a bark-like laugh and hurried steps back towards the door. The door opened quickly.

It was as if all of the school's once-glorious furnishings had been gathered in this one room and then forgotten. The rich, succulent colors of the various tapestries had grown stale and dull; magnificent paintings both hanging on the walls and standing on the floor had grown dark and murky; and where there had once been glorious plants and flowers, now stood only empty pots and vases.

The old man shuffled closer to the large desk that occupied most of the wall furthest away from the door and spoke to the man in the large wingback chair, his back turned towards them. There was another bark of laughter, and the chair swung around to face them. The man's expression instantly went from a wild grin to a scowl.

"Well, where is he? I don't see him! You said the boy was here!" He hammered his fist on the desk.

The old man looked to Barlow and Cletus.

Barlow remained confident. "He's inside the can, sir," he said, knocking on the tinman's chest with pride. There was a moment of tension as the man behind the desk glared at him. Then, just as quickly as the man had scowled at him, he smiled excitedly.

"Inside the can? He's inside the can? You can do that?" the man asked.

"Yes, sir, Mr. Purchase, sir," answered Barlow. Cletus nodded frantically.

Mr. Purchase flinched at the mention of his own name.

"It's a feature that has proved to be very useful of late," Barlow continued.

"He's inside the can, Mr. Brown! Inside the can!" Mr. Purchase half-sang to the old man. He leapt out from behind his desk, and it looked to Ben like he was almost skipping towards him, like a happy child.

"What on earth did he do to deserve that?" Mr. Purchase asked, rapping his knuckles on the tinman's chest playfully. "Did he misbehave?"

"You could say that, yes," said Barlow. "He tried to run away."

"Run away? How naughty! Run away, you say?" Mr. Purchase stood on his tiptoes and peered into the eyeholes. Ben jerked his head away.

"Well, we best get him out of there, shouldn't we? Make his acquaintance and all, don't you think? Let's not be rude."

"The boss said—" Cletus objected, before Barlow could stop him.

"I'm the only boss here!" Mr. Purchase roared, pushing past the tinman and grabbing Cletus. "You're in my house now, and you will do as I say. Why? Because I am the boss!" Cletus was flung to the floor like old rubbish, almost landing right inside the dark fireplace. Mr. Purchase spoke again, like nothing had happened.

"Let's open him up, shall we?" He clapped his hands together in excitement.

"Yes, Mr. Purchase," Barlow said. Mr. Purchase flinched again.

Barlow set to work as Mr. Purchase stared intently. As soon as the tinman's chest sprang open, he said, "Let's have a look-see, shall we?"

Ben was unceremoniously pulled out of the tinman. The tape was ripped off his mouth, and Barlow poked his fingers in to remove the gag as Ben was made to stand for a full inspection.

"Is this him? Is this him?" Mr. Purchase said. "Oh, very good! Smells a bit, doesn't he? And there's not much to him, is there? Oh, but he best behave himself here, or there won't be anything left of him. But now, do tell me, where's his hair?"

Ben wondered what Mr. Purchase could be talking about and tentatively put his hand to his head, where he felt nothing but the bristles of his newly-shorn hair. He had not known it had been cut off. He had endured so much in the last few hours, but them cutting his hair off was the last straw. He gnashed his teeth together, determined not to let these men see him cry.

"Good job on his hair, men! Where *is* his hair?" Mr. Purchase asked.

"It's been cut off, boss." Cletus was eager to please.

"I can see that! I'm not blind in the eye like my brother!" The windows rattled slightly as he yelled. Barlow turned his head towards Cletus and lowered his voice.

"Just shut up from now on, okay? Shut. *Up.*" He turned to face Mr. Purchase again. "We cut his hair off, boss, to make him look less like himself. It was a precaution."

"Smart, smart," Mr. Purchase said, as he thought it over. "And where is it now?"

"We burned it, boss, as soon as it was–" Barlow tried to answer.

"Burned it?" Purchase snarled. "Burned it? Why?"

"We were told to, sir," Cletus said, forgetting Barlow's order and regretting it immediately. Barlow clenched his teeth in frustration.

"Told to do so by whom?"

Neither of them responded.

"Answer me, man!" Mr. Purchase shouted.

"The other Mr. Purchase, sir!"

Another flinch.

"That half-wit brother of mine told you to burn it? What's the big idea?"

"He didn't want to leave any traces, sir!" Barlow answered. "He thought it would be best to take the extra precaution."

"Best, eh? Best? My brother thought it best?" His glare went from Barlow to Cletus. And then, suddenly, as if a switch had been flipped, he eased off. Cletus gave a big sigh of relief. "He always does think about what's best, doesn't he? Best…yes, I can see that." He mulled over the idea in his head. Then he focused on Ben again. "Still, let's have a look at him, let's have a good look."

He brought his face so close to Ben's that Ben thought Mr. Purchase wanted to smell him rather than look at him. Ben wanted to step back, but Barlow held him in place. Ben could count the number of little black hairs sprouting from Mr. Purchase's nostrils. With eyes bulging from their sockets, he inspected what felt like every inch of Ben's face.

"So, boy! Who do you look like – your ma or your pa? Huh? Huh? Ma or pa, which is it?"

Ben hesitated.

"Boy?" Mr. Purchase warned. The floor creaked as he inched even closer to him.

"My m-mother," Ben answered softly.

"Speak up, man!" Mr. Purchase ordered.

"My mother! I look like my mother."

"Pretty, is she?" he asked with a grin.

Ben was suddenly overwhelmed by images of his mother – her blonde hair always neat, her blue eyes always bright. He remembered the small things, like the fact that she always wore a string of pearls – a reminder of her own mother, she said. All of these things made Ben not want to answer. Talking about his mother's beauty to this man felt like a betrayal.

"Is she pretty?" Mr. Purchase screamed, and picked Ben clean off his feet. Mr. Brown rushed towards them as Mr. Purchase turned to face the window.

"Shh, shh… Easy, sir, easy. Remember, we need this one! We need to be extra careful with this one, sir! We can't break him. Now, answer him, boy," he said quickly and kindly. "Now!"

"Yes, she's pretty!" Ben said.

"Yes, who?"

"Yes, sir!"

Ben was dropped as Mr. Purchase turned back around to face Barlow and Cletus, who immediately looked away. "What about this thing?" he asked, nudging the tinman with his foot. "Does it still work?"

"I wouldn't bet on it, sir," Barlow said. "Nothing to keep the pendulum going now, I'm afraid."

"Pity, I could have used something like it here; we're a bit short-staffed. Still, I have Mr. Brown and the dogs. I guess they'll have to do for now…" He slowly turned and walked back behind his desk. When he was far enough away, Barlow ventured to speak.

"Will that be all from us then, sir?"

"Oh, you're not staying for dinner?" he asked, completely pleasant.

The question surprised Barlow. He seemed extremely careful in how he answered.

"Thank you, sir. But, no." He tried to sound grateful.

"Unfortunately, there is another job the other Mr. Purchase would like for us to do."

"He works you too hard," Mr. Purchase sighed. Then he said, "Very well, that is all."

"We may go, sir?" Barlow double-checked.

"Yes. And tell my baby brother that things are taken care of here. Things are well taken care of."

Chapter 6

A Twisted Oliver

As Barlow and Cletus left the house, Ben was lead down another series of staircases and hallways by Mr. Brown. Walking felt good, and he had to fight the urge to turn on his heels and run away. He had no idea where he was. He couldn't simply make a run for it because he had to assess the situation first. That was something his father had taught him to do.

Aside from the creaking of their footsteps, the house was eerily quiet. Where were all the other children? This was an orphanage, wasn't it? Surely there had to be more children! Ben couldn't decide whether or not he would be happy to come across any.

He was finally brought to a room in the basement, where he was told he would be staying. When his eyes adjusted to the gloom, he saw that the room was long and narrow, with about a dozen metal beds lined up like piano keys. Most carried a load of tattered and dirty bedding.

"Take one that's not got an occupant," Mr. Brown told him. "The boys will introduce themselves."

"How do I know which one is empty?" Ben asked.

"It'll be one without any blankets," Mr. Brown said, and left, shutting the door behind him.

This place might well have been the inspiration for *Oliver Twist*, Ben thought grimly. When he heard Mr. Brown's footsteps disappearing down the hallway, Ben got up from where he was sitting on one of the beds and opened the door a crack to see if the hallway was empty. Satisfied that he would be alone for a while, he began to inspect the room for means of escape. He listened for the sounds of the city, but he couldn't hear anything. Who knew how far they had traveled. They were undoubtedly miles away. Would he be able to get back?

His first idea was to climb through a window, but he saw that they were very narrow and too high up, like horizontal slits in the stone. Even if he could fit through one, he would have to climb onto something to reach them, and apart from the beds, there was nothing in the room to stack.

So, the only option he had was on the inside, but with all of the dark, maze-like stairwells and hallways, there was no telling where he would end up, or what – or who – he would come across.

No, something else, Ben thought. There must be another way out. A short gust of wind from behind him made him turn around. Against the far wall was the massive hearth of an old, unused fireplace. An idea struck him. He went closer. Cold air blew against his face as he looked up inside the fireplace, and when he couldn't see anything, he reached his hand inside and felt for the lintel, pulling down on the little ledge to see if it would support his weight.

"I wouldn't try that way, pal," said a voice from out of nowhere.

Ben leapt back from the fireplace as if he had been burned by it and looked around, trying to find whoever had spoken to him.

"Pardon?" His eyes sprang from shadow to shadow.

"Colin went up there a few weeks ago and didn't find the way out."

"So?"

"He didn't come back down either."

"He might have gotten out, then. How do you know he didn't?"

"I know because the dogs are still hungry."

The gory meaning sunk in as a boy finally stepped out from the shadows. He was about Ben's age, but a bit taller and skinnier, with a mop of brown hair.

"There are dogs?" Ben asked.

"Well, what Purchase likes to call dogs."

"And they eat…" Ben couldn't finish the sentence.

The boy nodded. Ben stepped away from the fireplace, as if the dogs might come out of it and grab him.

"Besides, Frankie says he heard Colin a few nights back, calling for help. Probably got stuck somewhere. It's easy when you don't know the way." After a few moments, he added, "You were lucky, you know."

"When? When was I lucky?"

"When you were upstairs, with Purchase."

"How was I lucky?"

"Purchase didn't throw you out of the window when you didn't answer about your mom being pretty or not. Mr. Brown must like you to help you like that."

"How do you know about that?" Ben asked, surprised.

"I was watching," he said.

There was a brief silence. Ben felt he was being inspected yet again.

"He throws people out of windows?"

"Only boys, and only when he gets really angry," the boy said casually. He walked closer to Ben. "It's happened twice now. Well, twice since I've been here."

Ben had a strong feeling that it hadn't just happened twice.

"My name's Mackenzie, by the way. Mackenzie White," he said, and stuck out his hand for Ben to shake.

"Ben." The two of them shook hands.

"Welcome to Sugarhill, pal."

"What is this place?" asked Ben, looking around the room again.

"Sugarhill? It's a school for boys. Well, it used to be. It's really just an orphanage now, only no one ever comes to adopt any of us. I doubt people even know we're here."

There was that word again: orphan. It was a heavy word, one that filled him with dread. Maybe all of it was true, he thought. No one aside from his parents and Olivander knew that he had come to America. And with his parents missing and Uncle Lucas allegedly dead, there was no one left to inform Olivander that he had been taken from his uncle's house. Would Mary think to alert someone? Maybe when she heard of her employer's death she would wonder what had happened to Ben. But who would she contact? The police? They already knew.

Ben felt his only hope was that Olivander would grow suspicious, after not hearing from Ben. He had promised to write, after all. Ben suddenly remembered the key to No. 4 and frantically tried to find it, afraid that it had been taken from him, or that he had managed to lose it. But it was still tucked safely inside his pocket, where it had always been. He squeezed it tightly in his hand.

"So who died and made you come to this place?" Mackenzie asked, as he plopped down on the nearest bed, its springs squeaking underneath him. Ben was surprised at how casually Mackenzie talked about death.

"My uncle, I guess, but I don't think he's dead," he answered.

"Trust me, pal, if you're here, then he's dead."

Ben's innards squirmed.

"Your uncle, huh? Your ma and pa dead?"

"No, they're not dead," Ben said quickly.

"Ah, one of those. Your ma and pa didn't want you?"

"No, it's not like that at all," he stammered. "It's complicated."

"Complicated? They're either dead or alive, there's nothing complicated about it."

"My mum and dad aren't dead, they're…doing something. I just can't be with them right now."

"So you're *here*?"

"I guess so."

After another silence, Mackenzie asked, "Where are you from, anyway?"

"London," answered Ben. "England."

"No way! Like Sherlock Holmes?" Mackenzie asked excitedly, jumping up from the bed. Ben cracked a smile.

"Yes, like Sherlock Holmes! Do you like him?"

"I've read all of his stories!"

"So have I!" Ben exclaimed.

"Wait, have you read *The Blue Carbuncle*?"

"Of course!"

"That is so amazing! No one here knows anything about Holmes and Watson. I've never met a British person before." The gears in Mackenzie's head sprang into overdrive. "But wait, if you're from England, why'd they bring you all the way to America just to put you in an orphanage? Don't you have orphanages in England?"

"I was visiting my uncle in New York City when I was brought here."

"Don't you have any other relatives?"

"Not in America, no. Although my grandfather did live here when he was a boy," he said, hoping that it might help answer Mackenzie's question.

"You're lucky. I don't have any relatives – none that are alive anymore, anyway. Do your relatives like you?"

"I hope so!" Ben said, with genuine surprise. He had never really thought about being liked by them.

"So why didn't you just go to them?"

"I wasn't given the option!"

"Surely they would ask about you when they heard of your uncle kicking it."

"Well, that only happened yesterday. But I don't think they'll know where to find me, anyway. Now no one aside from Olivander knows that I'm even here, in America, I mean."

"Who's Olivander?"

"He's our, um, butler, I guess. But he's more than–"

"You have a butler?" Mackenzie asked, in awe.

Ben nodded.

"But, so, anyway, even if your folks were dead, you still wouldn't be in here! How come those men brought you here?"

"I don't know."

"Well, didn't they say anything?" Mackenzie pressed.

"Not much! All I know is that my uncle went to his office

yesterday morning, and then he didn't come back, and a policeman and two men showed up at his house with a very nasty tinman. They wouldn't tell me how he died, only that he had. The next thing I know, I'm here! And I thought the police were supposed to help people."

"Oh. *Him*," Mackenzie said. "That was probably Cletus. No, he's not a normal policeman, he wouldn't do you any favors. Not while he's hanging out with that Barlow guy. That one is a piece of work. Real nasty. He works for the other M—"

"The man with the one white eye?" Ben interrupted.

"Yes! How do you know about him?" Mackenzie asked.

"He was there at the house, too."

Mackenzie seemed taken aback by this. "Mr. Purchase was at your house?"

"No, of course not. I don't mean him. I only just met him here."

"Not this Mr. Purchase, the *other* Mr. Purchase," Mackenzie said, his voice becoming a whisper.

"There are two of them?"

"They're brothers. The one with the eye is supposed to be the baby brother, though you wouldn't know it." He leaned in close. "Mr. Purchase was at your house, to come and get you personally?"

"I suppose so," Ben said.

"Wow. He must've really wanted to get his hands on you."

"Is that a bad thing?"

"I hear that Mr. Purchase never does anything like

57

that – he's got men to do the muscle work for him. Men like Barlow, real nasty."

"How do you know all this?"

"I listen. I hide in the walls, and I listen."

Mackenzie stepped closer to Ben and lowered his voice even more. "Mr. Purchase is a bad guy." Mackenzie looked around as if to see if anybody else might be listening. "And if he told you your uncle is dead, then your uncle is dead."

A shiver ran down Ben's spine. And he knew it had to be his imagination, but it suddenly felt a lot colder in the room.

He realized that his parents and Uncle Lucas must have gotten it all wrong. They had called him "The Buyer" when his name was actually Mr. Purchase! A silly mistake, but a mistake nonetheless. And while his parents were trying to find Mr. Purchase, Mr. Purchase had found Ben instead! He was whom they had wanted to keep him safe from, but they had inadvertently delivered him almost personally by bringing him to America. Ben couldn't help but stand in awe of the whole situation. Not only had he met The Buyer, but he had also lived to tell the tale. If only he could get news to his parents that he knew both The Buyer's real name and where he was.

"No wonder the real police weren't there," Mackenzie continued. "Not with Mr. Purchase running things. Say, you don't think your parents might also have, you know, run into Mr. Purchase?"

"No," he said, after giving it some quick thought. "My parents left the country two days ago. They got onto a ship and everything. Or rather, I was told that they did."

Everything else seemed to have been a lie, why shouldn't that have been one as well? But Ben reckoned that the only reason Mr. Purchase would want him would be as a bartering tool to use against his mum and dad, to make them stop what they were doing. He wouldn't need him if there was no one to barter with, if his mum and dad were already dead.

Mackenzie thought for a while. "Ben, I think you're in a lot of trouble," he said gravely. "Do you think you've been kidnapped?" And like a lightning bolt had hit his head, he said, "Ah, that's it! You've been kidnapped! Just like with Sherlock Holmes and that boy in *The Priory School Adventure*! And you know what that means, don't you? It means that somebody wants something in exchange for you!" Mackenzie had hit the nail on the head.

"Something like what?" Ben asked, knowing full well.

"I don't know. In the story they wanted the Duke of Holdernesse to change his will. Could that be it? Maybe Mr. Purchase wants your parents to change their will? Are you very wealthy? Oh, maybe that's it. Maybe they just want you for some money. I mean, is there anything else they could be after?"

"Not that I can think of," Ben lied. He thought about Liza, wondering if the same fate had befallen her. Maybe she was being held for ransom, too.

Ben sighed dejectedly.

"I have to get to Liza. I have to get out of here," he said quietly to himself.

"Okay," Mackenzie said matter-of-factly.

"Okay? You mean it's possible?"

"Yeah, it's possible."

Ben looked at him in awe. "Then why haven't you ever escaped?"

"I know how to do it, and I have thought about it, but I don't really have anywhere else to go," Mackenzie said, shrugging. "At least here I've got a bed, and they do feed us. Every now and then Mr. Brown even gives us some cake."

"But you do know how to?"

"I sure do."

"And can you show me?"

"Well, if I were you, I wouldn't want to wait here for Mr. Purchase to decide what to do with me either. It won't be anything good."

"So you'll help me? You can get me out?"

"Sure I can. But keeping you alive while I do it is going to be a bit more difficult."

Chapter 7

THE HUNTED HOUSE

The dark figure had skulked in the city shadows since sunset, his eyes trained on the unlit house across from him. Occasionally his view became obscured by a horse and carriage, or a car passing in the street, but for the most part he was able to see the entirety of Lucas Bashford's house from where he stood. He was hoping to see movement inside it – anything from the flutter of a curtain to the darkening of a shadow, anything that might indicate life. No movement, no matter how slight, would go unnoticed by him.

So far, nothing in the house had so much as stirred, and he had not been given any hope that anyone remained in the house – anyone who'd be able to tell him where the boy and his uncle had gone.

This annoyed him, and he didn't like being annoyed.

A short while later, having made certain that no one else was watching the house, he sprinted across the street. Then, with the help of his rubber-lined hands, he effortlessly scaled the fence, missing the passing beams of a car's headlights by mere seconds. Moving from shadow to shadow, he moved to the rear of the house, where there was no chance of being seen from the street. He took one last look inside the house before knocking out a pane of glass right above the door lock.

Chapter 8

OUT OF THE FRYING PAN AND INTO THE FIREPLACE

"There's a whistle," Mackenzie said quietly.

He had made sure the other boys were still nowhere near their room before he began. "There's a whistle that calls the dogs. Purchase lets them roam the woods and only calls them back for the occasional feeding. When he's got something – or someone – to get rid of, he calls them by using the whistle. I've seen it twice now, and I know what it looks like. If we can get it and then get you out of the house safely, I could blow it, to lure the dogs back to the house and away from where you're running, long enough for you to get away."

"Won't you get in trouble?"

Mackenzie thought about this for a second.

"Only if they find out it was me," he smiled devilishly. "And then only if they find me. Besides, I'd like to help a friend."

"We're friends?"

Mackenzie regarded Ben for a few seconds. "You seem like an all right guy. And you're from England. I've never had an English friend before." Mackenzie smiled. "You'll remember me when you're back in England, right?"

"Of course I will. And I'll tell my parents about this place so they can help."

"You have to find them first, so we'd better get started. I need to draw you a map. It's only a couple of hours until sunset."

"I'm leaving tonight?"

"Yes! The longer you stay the more difficult it will be for you to leave. And Purchase won't expect anything tonight – he won't think you'll try to escape so soon! He won't know you know how to get out!"

"But how do we get the whistle?"

"The chimney."

"The chimney? But I thought you said people got stuck up there. What about Colin?"

"If he was still in there, I would have found him ages ago. Personally, I think Frankie is full of it. Who knows what happened to Colin."

"Oh," Ben said, slightly relieved.

"People still get stuck up there though, but only when

they go too far, or don't know the way. If you know the way like I do, you can go almost anywhere in the house, even right into Purchase's office. How do you think I was able to see you?"

"Is that where you were, in the fireplace?"

Mackenzie nodded.

"Aren't you scared of getting burned?"

"Oh, that fireplace hasn't worked in years. I think the chimney must be blocked or something."

"And how are we going to get the whistle without being seen?"

"Purchase leaves his office for supper. I'll get the whistle while he is downstairs."

"But won't someone know you're missing?"

"Neither Purchase nor Mr. Brown has ever minded anyone missing dinner. 'The fewer that eat, the better,' they say. I'll be okay. Now, let's make you a map."

Ben sat alongside Mackenzie as he drew in the waning afternoon light, Mackenzie talking as he went along, explaining the details of the area. The map showed Ben the road that lead from the school down towards the train tracks that led to a little station where stock trains were said to stop to pick up goods. One of those trains would take him right back into New York City, Mackenzie told him. All he had to do was get on one.

Ben sat alone at dinner that night, conscious of the stares

from the other boys. No one else had dared speak to him. No one else was as forthcoming, or even as curious as Mackenzie had been. And Ben couldn't decide whether an attempt to introduce himself to another boy would jeopardize his chances of escape or not.

The boys varied in age from about four to thirteen. They ate in absolute silence. Ben followed suit and ate what little he had been given, keeping his head low, thinking about Mackenzie. And even though he was worried, it made Ben feel better to see Mr. Purchase sitting at the main table, right in front of him. At least Mr. Purchase was here and not in his office where he could catch Mackenzie. Ben watched as Mr. Purchase greedily forked large amounts of food into his mouth, ignoring everyone around him as he did. As long as he had enough to eat he was quiet, a trick Mr. Brown tended to with great efficiency. The inviting smell of his meat and potatoes wafted over the boys, making the porridge they had been given even more unappetizing.

Halfway through dinner, Mr. Purchase looked up at Ben and gave him a crooked, knowing smile, his mouth shiny from the grease and gravy. He snorted a laugh before returning to his food.

The boys had long been done with their dinner by the time Mr. Purchase finally finished eating. They weren't allowed to leave before then, and as soon as he pushed his chair back from the table, the boys stood in unison. Ben stayed out of the way, trailing behind the last few boys as they made their way into the hall. He was stopped near the door by Mr. Brown.

"You get used to the food eventually," he said, not unkindly. "It's either that or starve." He handed Ben a rolled-up blanket, but before Ben could thank him, Mr. Brown walked away to clear Mr. Purchase's plate.

The boys split into two groups and went to their respective bedrooms. Ben followed cautiously, and when he walked into the room his new roommates showed no reaction to his presence. He wondered if Mackenzie had any friends that might know something, whether Mackenzie trusted anybody else in this place. But there was no way to find out.

None of the boys seemed to care that one of their roommates was missing. What they were interested in was the unused blankets on the bed. The short scrap over whose blanket it was to become was half-hearted and dull, the victorious boy simply turning his back on the rest before crawling into his own bed. Ben noticed that no one changed into pajamas before getting into bed. No one even took off their shoes.

Down the hall, Mr. Brown banged on a pot with a wooden spoon, and the candle was extinguished.

Ben lay in his bed, wondering and worrying. The moon was full and bright, making it a good night to leave.

He thought about what time it was, about how long Mackenzie had been gone. Then, fed up with feeling helpless, he sat up in bed, determined to find Mackenzie even if it meant venturing into the flues. A hand suddenly took him by the shoulder. Ben's head snapped back to see Mackenzie grinning at him, the whistle held out for him to see.

"Follow me," he whispered, "and bring your blanket."

"Why? Where are we going?"

"You'll see. We're going back up into the flues. There's a way into what used to be a ballroom. You can get out from there!"

Ben pulled the blanket from his bed and followed Mackenzie closely, constantly checking that no one in the room had woken up and seen them. They reached the hearth, and he watched as Mackenzie stepped inside and climbed up into the chimney. Taking one last look around the room, Ben ducked and stepped in, slowly straightening up so as to not bump his head.

"Put your foot up on the lintel there," instructed Mackenzie from above. "Then climb up onto the smoke shelf."

Ben pushed his back against the wall to gain some leverage and used his legs, inching his way up into the darkness. He was soon sitting on the smoke shelf, grateful for the light coming from the stubby candle Mackenzie had lit. Then, using the uneven slabs of stone as ladder rungs, he followed Mackenzie further into the flue.

A few feet up, they crawled along into a horizontal opening, and Mackenzie blew out the candle. It was now pitch black.

"Why'd you do that?" Ben asked in a whisper.

"I don't want anyone to see us coming."

Ben tensed up. Mackenzie's voice suddenly seemed a lot farther away than he thought it should have been. He crawled closer and touched Mackenzie's foot. Every now and then, Ben moved too fast, bumping into Mackenzie. Other times he moved too slow, making him think he had lost Mackenzie forever in the maze of soot.

It was the moonlight that finally indicated the end of their route: the opening of the fireplace in the ballroom. Ben could feel the cold wind pushing past them, wind that came in through the broken panes of glass in the un-boarded windows that stood from floor to ceiling. Sheer curtains, worn and torn through years of neglect and rough weather, swayed like strung ghosts.

"Now, if you were to climb up that one there," said Mackenzie, pointing to another fireplace on the far wall, "it'd take you right up to Purchase's office on the next floor." He seemed proud to know this. Ben nodded.

"By the way, what's the blanket for?" Ben asked.

"The train journey. It's going to get very cold on that train," he said. His answer was followed by a moment of silence as the two boys looked at each other.

"Well, I guess this is it." Mackenzie gave Ben the map he had drawn and made sure he fully understood the directions. Then he reached into the fireplace and took a fist full of soot.

"What's that for?" Ben asked.

"It's camouflage. The moon is really bright tonight, and the darker you are, the harder it will be to see you from the house." He rubbed some of the soot onto Ben's face, Ben having just enough time to shut his eyes. He dusted some onto Ben's head and then rubbed more on the back of his neck.

"There," Mackenzie said, as he inspected the result, satisfied.

"I'm worried that you will get in trouble," said Ben.

"I'll only get in trouble if they find me, and they won't. I'll be okay in the flues. They can't get to me when I'm in there. The important thing is to get you away. Now, it takes about twenty minutes to get to the main road. I'll give you five before I call the dogs, and by the time they get here and realize there's no food, you'll be too far gone for them to catch up. Run on the side of the driveway, never in the middle. The grass will muffle your footsteps."

"And when I get to the gate?" he asked, when he saw it on the map.

"It won't be a problem. There's not much left of the wall that surrounds it, so getting over it should be easy."

When Mackenzie couldn't think of anything else to say, or any more advice or directions to give, he stuck out his hand and waited for Ben to take it. "Good luck," he said.

The reality of leaving Sugarhill suddenly left Ben with a feeling of unexpected sadness. He was surprised by the feeling, but knew it wasn't Sugarhill that he didn't want to leave, it was Mackenzie. He had found a friend, one who had made the last twenty-four hours less unnerving, and he didn't want to say goodbye to yet another person. But he knew that if he didn't, things would only get worse.

"Come with me," he said suddenly.

"What?" Mackenzie asked, surprised.

"Come with me. Don't stay here. You said yourself that you don't have anyone left in America. You can come to England with me. My parents will take care of you."

"You don't even know where your parents are!"

"Then we can find them together. You can help me. Mackenzie, come with me," Ben pressed.

Mackenzie looked out the windows at the midnight sky, thinking. "I would live with you in England?"

"Yes!"

"With you and your family?"

"We can even share a room, like brothers."

Mackenzie smiled. "That would be nice."

"Then come with me."

Mackenzie smiled again, and for a second Ben was convinced that he was going to go with him. But then Mackenzie looked down and said, "I want to, but I can't. What about the whistle, Ben? We can't both run; the dogs will get us. If I don't stay here to blow the whistle, neither one of us will make it out safely."

"But…"

"I'd really like to do all that. To come with you and help find your family and all, but I need to stay here and blow the whistle."

Ben knew that what Mackenzie was saying made sense, and it made him feel worse.

"Then make me a promise," Ben said earnestly. "Promise me that you'll stay out of trouble."

Mackenzie nodded his head.

"I promise to come back for you," Ben said.

"Then I better not go anywhere," Mackenzie added awkwardly. "Good luck, Ben."

"Thank you. Good luck to you, too."

Chapter 9

THE WEASEL CHASED THE MONKEY

Ben raced down the side of the road as fast as he could, the cold night air biting at his nose and knuckles. The birch trees loomed high above him, their white branches gently swaying in the breeze like skeletal fingers waving at the moon. Mackenzie had been right about running on the side of the driveway. His footsteps were barely audible, the damp, dead grass serving to cushion his footfalls. He had also been right about the moon. It was very bright indeed and caused Ben concern about patches of clean skin that Mackenzie might have missed with the soot.

He pictured Mackenzie making his way into the foyer to the grandfather clock, watching intently for the allotted time to pass. How long had it been since Ben had left the house? Had it been five minutes yet?

His heart leapt up into his throat, and his skin froze when a dog bark sounded in the distance. It seemed far enough away at first, but when the second bark came, it was a lot louder and a lot closer than before. Soon there was a rapid succession of barks, each sounding more savage and closer than the first.

He heard movement close by, twigs snapping and dead leaves rustling as the bushes were disturbed. He pushed himself to run faster, trying desperately to ignore the voice in his head that told him he was about to be mauled. His heart was pounding in his ears like a double drum set, his chest burning, his brow wet with sweat. He strained his ears to listen for any approaching signs of danger. That's when he heard the long, piercing sound of the whistle. He stopped running briefly to look back at the house. A light had gone on.

Purchase was awake.

Ben had no idea how close to the main road he was, but he knew that he had to keep going and keep at it as hard as he could because if he was caught, all of Mackenzie's efforts would have been for nothing. And a second escape would be next to impossible. He kept running.

Anyone unfortunate enough to hear Mr. Purchase snore would say it sounded like two dry and craggy boulders, laboriously scraping against each other, first one way for the inhale, then the other way for the exhale. This was cut short when the screaming dog whistle woke him up.

At first Mr. Purchase remained in his bed, hollering for Mr. Brown. When he didn't get the speedy and appropriately apologetic response he wanted, he flung off his bed covers and stormed to the window.

"Will you shut up?" he yelled at the dogs barking outside. "Mr. Brown!" he roared, as different scenarios as to what might have happened raced through his mind. "Someone's stolen my whistle! And one of our birds wants to learn how to fly!" With that, he stormed downstairs, half-singing, half-shouting an old nursery rhyme in an attempt to frighten the boys.

"All around the mulberry bush, the monkey chased the weasel…" He barreled down the steps, taking them two by two, "The monkey thought 'twas all in…" misjudged the final step and tripped. He froze, looking to see if anyone had heard or seen him. When he was convinced that he had been unobserved, he turned and kicked open the door to the first boys' room, marching inside.

"Mis-ter Brown!" he summoned again, his voice cracking.

Mr. Brown finally came running towards him, skidding to a halt. "Yes, sir?"

"Light the lights, and let's see which little bird has flown our nest."

Mr. Brown cleared his throat. "There are no lights in here, sir."

"What?" he demanded.

"There are no lights down here, sir."

"Why not?"

"'What do they need with light?' you said. 'It's a waste of money,' you said."

"Then bring me something!" he cried, exasperated.

Mr. Brown scurried away, returning moments later with a lit candelabrum. The boys were ordered to get up and stand in front of their beds.

"Count them, Mr. Brown," Mr. Purchase instructed.

Mr. Brown did as he was told. "They're all here, sir," he said eventually.

"Every bed taken?"

"Every bed, sir," he confirmed.

"Then it must be one of the other ones!" he shouted, as he ran out of the room. Mr. Brown followed hastily, fumbling with his keys to unlock the next door. But Mr. Purchase had gotten there first and proceeded to kick it open as well. "Count them, man! Count them!"

Mr. Brown darted around the room, counting. "There's one missing, sir," he said finally.

Standing in front of his bed, Mackenzie was trying hard to control his breathing. He had run as fast as he could to make it back downstairs in time.

"One missing, eh? Any idea who it – wait! Where's the Bloomswell boy?"

Mr. Brown's face fell. "Surely he wouldn't have tried it, sir.

Not already!"

"Where is he?" Mr. Purchase insisted.

Mr. Brown searched every boy's face, bringing the candles close in order to have a good look at each and every one of them. Eventually he said, "Not here, sir."

Mr. Purchase did not look well. Even in the dim light you could see that all the color had drained from his face. "Send the hounds out again," he said finally.

Mr. Brown was surprised at the order. "Sir?"

"Perhaps they've found his sister by now. Perhaps they don't need him anymore. Besides, the parents need not know he's dead," he said.

With a nod to confirm he meant what he said, Mr. Purchase made for the door. Just before he walked out, he felt a cold breeze coming from the fireplace. He glanced towards it and smiled when he saw the ash footprints leading from it.

Chapter 10

STOWAWAY THE RUNAWAY

Ben slid between two large crates – the two large crates that seemed the least likely to move and crush him when the train started up. He pulled his legs in close, trying to make himself as small and as inconspicuous as possible. Then he tucked the tattered blanket tightly around himself and waited for the train to resume its journey. He figured Mr. Purchase had probably discovered that he was missing by now, and since he seemed to be without car or horse and carriage, the other Mr. Purchase, back in New York City, had probably been informed of the situation. He hoped Mackenzie was safe.

He thought about the journey ahead of him. Getting back to the city now seemed simple enough, but what would he do when he got there? Where would he go? Could he go back to his uncle's house? Or would there be somebody there waiting for him?

No, Ben thought. A trip back to his uncle's house would be like walking straight back into Sugarhill. He would have to get help and find out what happened to his uncle some other way. And since one of his kidnappers apparently worked for the police, that was out of the question, too. Where else could he go? He had to get back to England somehow.

The rhythmic swaying of the train soon rocked Ben into a deep, dreamless sleep. He only woke up when the train came to a noisy stop at the depot a few hours later. For a brief moment, right when he opened his eyes, Ben forgot where he was and everything seemed right with the world.

Then he sat up sharply and listened for any signs of danger. He peered out through the slats of wood on the side of the car, to see if the coast was clear, but all he could see was the back of another train car.

He assumed someone would start unloading the crates soon, and he knew he would have to get off of the train before he was discovered. Nevertheless, Ben needed more time to come up with a plan. He had managed to get back into the city, but he had no idea what to do next. He was angry at himself for falling asleep when he should have been thinking of a way to get home. How *was* he going to get back to England? He couldn't return on the *La Bourgogne*. Aside from the fact that it would take him back to France and not to London, he didn't have any money to buy passage on such a fancy vessel – his lack of money meant that traveling by airship was also out of the question.

On top of that, the only people he knew in America wanted him dead, or were dead themselves, which meant there was no one to ask for help.

Had all of this happened in England he would have had many recourses. He could have simply gone to Olivander for help, or contacted his grandparents, or even gone to his school.

Here, he was completely alone.

Had his parents been able to contact Olivander? If so, maybe he had been able to help Liza. But there was no way to know for sure, so Ben had to go to Liza himself.

Tucking himself back among the taller crates again, he made himself comfortable and thought about what to do next. It was then that his stomach started to rumble, and Ben was suddenly struck by a thought: There might be something to eat in one of the crates!

He hopped down to read the first label, but was quickly disappointed. There was nothing but drive-rivets inside. The next crate contained spools of unbleached wool, the one after that, reams of paper. He moved from one crate to the next, reading label after label, but not one held anything for him to eat.

Disheartened, he stared at the crates and their labels, and as his mind wandered again, a single word slowly stood out from the rest. He touched the rough lettering to make sure he hadn't imagined it. He felt silly for not noticing such a valuable detail before. The contents of the crate had proved to be unhelpful, but its destination would be. He had the next step to his plan. It involved getting to the harbor to find *The Queen Fredericka*. Her destination, according to the crate?

London, England.

Chapter 11

BEGGARS CAN'T BE CRUISERS

Ben was amazed at how many people simply ignored him when he asked them for directions to the harbor, some not even pausing to hear what it was he wanted. Those who didn't automatically throw coins at him probably *thought* that money was what he wanted and also gave him a wide berth. No one had ever reacted this way to him before. Maybe Americans were simply rude.

He was again attempting to get the attention of passersby when he noticed a reflection in a shop window. Ben did a double-take. For a second he hadn't recognized himself. He looked like a street urchin, not like Benjamin Sebastian Bloomswell. His hair was gone, his skin was grungy under a layer of day-old soot, and his clothes were dirtier than they had ever been before. He stood like that, staring at himself, for some time. Then, giving the key to No. 4 a reassuring pat, he took a deep breath and turned away from his reflection. He looked a state, both to himself and to passersby, but certainly directions weren't too much to ask for, regardless of who was asking.

Suddenly, out of nowhere, someone seized him by his collar, dragged him into the first accessible alley and pinned him up against the wall. Ben could almost see Sugarhill again, but was soon overwhelmed by the rank breath of his assailant.

"What's the big idea, trespassing on my territory?" the man snarled.

Ben turned his face away to avoid the incredible stench coming from the man, who was baring what little was left of his teeth.

"I'm sorry! I'm sorry! I didn't know!"

"A likely story!" the man barked, increasing his grip. "The gall, taking money off of my streets!"

"I wasn't asking them for money! I was asking for directions. Honestly!"

"Directions? Ha! Directions? And where would you need directions to, pray tell? Fifth Avenue? Or perhaps a museum!" He guffawed.

"No, to the harbor!" Ben interjected.

"Oh, the harbor, is it? What do you want the harbor for? Going on a cruise? Setting out to sea?"

"Yes," Ben said.

"Oh." The man's face relaxed slightly. "So you weren't trying to move into my area?"

"No, sir."

"Ha! 'Sir.' I like that. I haven't been called that in years. 'Sir.'" He rolled the word around in his mouth. His grip on Ben lessened, and Ben tried to move away from the stench a tad bit. But he moved too quickly, and the man's grip tightened. He eyed him suspiciously, his eye twitching again.

"Directions, hmm? To the harbor? They drown rats like you at the harbor, you know."

"They probably do, sir."

"Ha! 'Sir.' I like that. I haven't been called that in years," he said dreamily.

"Yes, sir."

"'Sir.' I like that." He eyed him for another moment. "I tell you what. You give me the money that was given to you on my property, and I'll give you directions off my property. Sound fair?"

"You'll give me directions to the harbor?"

"I said, 'directions off my property.' If that leads you to the harbor, well, then I guess you're just a lucky boy, aren't you?"

"Yes," Ben said, and added, "sir." Just to be on the safe side.

"'Sir.' Yes, I do like that."

Ben followed the garbled directions he'd been given between the counting and the recounting of the few coins he'd handed over. And to his utmost surprise, about an hour and a half later, he found himself looking at the collection of cargo ships anchored in the harbor.

He spent some time looking for *The Queen Fredericka* and finally spotted the rusted red and white cargo ship lazing at the end of Pier 3. When he saw that ramps were still set for cargo to be loaded, he knew that his luck was changing.

All he had to do now was to wait till nightfall and sneak aboard.

Just then, his stomach rumbled again. He had been able to ignore its pangs all day, but it seemed his stomach had had more than enough of this neglect. He should have bought something to eat with the money he'd been thrown.

His hunger soon brought more concerns. The excitement of his seemingly brilliant plan abandoned him, leaving only its flaws. Here he was, about to stow away on a vessel bound for England, without so much as a morsel of food to tide him over – much less enough for the entire journey – and who knew exactly how long it would take? Adrenaline had pushed him this far, but he knew that two or three weeks without any food would be impossible. He considered the possibility of stealing food from the crew, but that would almost certainly lead to discovery. Who knew what would happen to him then, what they would do?

On top of everything, he now felt stupid. Stupid for ever thinking that sailing to England was the answer. He had been so convinced that it was his only option. And, well, maybe it was. He had to make it work somehow.

Could he persuade the captain of *The Queen Fredericka* to take him on as a deckhand or scullion? He could tell the captain he would work for his passage.

But what if after he introduced himself to the captain, he was turned down? It might be extra difficult to stow away if the captain was fully aware that someone wanted a free ride.

Then again, if he didn't make a big deal of specifically going to England, made it sound as if the purpose of his wanting to sail with *The Queen Fredericka* was employment and to have the opportunity to learn to be a sailor, he might stand a better chance.

He figured that he needed to make a good impression with the captain when he met him. Ben had been told quite often by his grandfather that first impressions lasted and were therefore very important. So Ben found steps leading to the water and splashed some against his face, trying to remove at least some of the dirt. He inspected his rippled reflection in the water. Not a vast improvement, but it was a start.

He climbed back up the steps and made for the ship.

Someone had other plans for Ben.

He was rammed with such force that both he and his attacker skidded a couple of feet along.

"You really have made this easy for me, you know?" Barlow said breathlessly. "Difficult for yourself, but easy for me. To think, I don't even have to drag you to your final resting place!"

Ben's head was swimming, and the weight of Barlow on top of him made struggle useless. How on earth had Barlow managed to catch him here?

"At least at Sugarhill you were safe! You might have lived to see your next birthday, even! But when you ran, they had to make other plans, didn't they? Lucky for us we don't really need you anymore, isn't it? Not so lucky for you, but it's lucky for us! No one needs to tell your father you're gone, right? He can keep on thinking we have you so that he does exactly what we say."

Ben tried to wriggle his way out from underneath Barlow.

"Not so fast! I'm not done with my story yet! Quite a troublemaker, aren't you? Only care about yourself, don't you? I realized that when you left your friend to fend for himself back at Sugarhill. Don't care much what happened to him, do you?"

Ben froze. Barlow was talking about Mackenzie!

"Well, let me tell you anyway! They followed his footsteps from the fireplace straight to his bed. And when he knew they were on to him, he ran and crawled back up the fireplace! He thought he could hide in the house, hide in the flues, didn't he? Well, they smoked him out good. They lit every fire in that place, near burned the whole thing down!" he said, laughing. Then something caught in his throat, and he started to cough.

"Never did come out, the little sneak," he said, between coughs. "He probably got lost and choked in the smoke. It wouldn't have been the first time that it happened. It is a pity really, there's good eating for the dogs there." He got up off of Ben and lifted him to his feet. He glanced over at the water. "I wonder if the fish feel the same?"

Ben did not see the blow coming. It came so fast and so hard that it spun him around through the air like a top. Ben's head, particularly his eye, felt like exploding. It was the voices in the distance that made Barlow look around, giving Ben just the chance he needed to get back to his feet. He ran towards the edge of the pier, moving completely on instinct.

He heard Barlow's angry shout, but before he could lay his hands on him, Ben dove off the edge of the pier and into the murky water.

It took a lot of effort for Ben to pull himself out of the water. He had managed to get away from Barlow and to keep a safe distance from him, hiding underneath another pier. But as he waited for Barlow to finally leave, he could feel his mind wander in a scary way. His head was becoming cloudy, the adrenaline subsiding, and he was struggling to stay in control of himself amidst the cotton balls that were filling his head. Where was he again? Why was he…wet?

His head was spinning. He climbed the rusty ladder and shuffled along the pier. Then he stumbled into a wooden crate, just like the ones he had hidden among on the train. This one's lid was half-off, inviting him to crawl in.

Chapter 12

WHERE THERE'S SMOKE

The dark figure stood in the shadows of the woods as he watched smoke rise from every single chimney of The Sugarhill School for Boys. He had not found anything useful at the house in the city. Upon arrival on the school's grounds he had been given a more than generous opportunity to vent his frustration when a pack of desperately ugly dogs sprang on him from several directions. Now, however, as he watched smoke billow into the darkening night sky, he found himself at odds about what to do. Fire, with its indiscriminate appetite, annoyed him.

Of course, smoke rising from a chimney was not uncommon, and was no real reason for concern, but something about what he saw did not sit right with him.

It was when he heard the scream that he sprang forward.

He would later find out that the boy he rescued was not the boy he had come for. And it would annoy him greatly.

Chapter 13

In the Company of the Queen

The flat end of the crowbar was rammed under the crate lid, lifting it lopsidedly by about half an inch. There was a dull thump as it was thrust in again, followed by the creaking of wood as the lid was forced open even more. One by one, the nails that had secured the lid down were pried from the wood, like roots grudgingly giving up their hold on the earth. As the lid finally lifted completely off, light came spilling into the crate, and two men peered in from above.

"I told you there was something else inside," said one of the men.

Ben, barely awake, was actually quite surprised to find himself alive. He was cramped and uncomfortable, but he was really quite cozy on top of the fabrics underneath him.

"What do we have here, a stowaway?" asked the other man, with a bit of a chuckle.

Ben's head was ringing, the man's voice echoing inside it like it a marble rolling around the inside of a cake pan.

The larger of the two men reached into the crate and took hold of Ben's shoulder. Ben was vaguely aware that he probably ought to prepare himself for some kind of fight, but the man was surprisingly gentle, pulling Ben up into a seated position.

"A stowaway?" he said. "Nah, by the looks of that shiner, I think he bought his passage fair and square." He inspected Ben's eye closely. "And judging by the size of it, he should be traveling first class."

Ben was still trying to make sense of what was going on. Where was he? Who were these men? "What's a shiner?" Ben mumbled, barely able to string the sentence together.

The men laughed, and together they lifted Ben out of the crate. A piece of mirror was held up for Ben to see, and when his vision came into focus he realized what he was looking at. His left eye was almost completely swollen shut, swallowed by a purple-black bruise.

"That, my boy, is a shiner," said the skinnier man. "And a proper one at that."

Ben blinked a few times, trying to focus on the bruise. Why was the earth moving like that?

"Easy there, easy. It'll take some time before you get your sea legs." The men helped him sit down on one of the smaller crates.

"Sea legs?" Ben asked unsteadily.

"Now, if you want to air your belly, here's a bucket all ready for you," said the thin man. "But in the meantime, do you think you can manage this?" He handed Ben a cup of steaming hot, milky tea. "It should make you feel better."

"I hope you like it sweet," the other man said.

The tea was glorious. Its warmth and sweetness flooded his mouth, washed over his dry, fuzzy tongue, and easily slipped down his throat. He only eased up when he needed to take a breath of air. He gasped, satisfied.

"Better?"

Ben nodded.

"Better get him a refill, Whip," the larger man said. The cup was handed over and refilled with tea.

"Do you think you can tell us who you are and what you are doing here now?" asked the man.

Before he answered, Ben swallowed another big mouthful of tea, examining their faces over the rim of the cup. He didn't seem to be in any kind of trouble, and the men seemed genuinely intrigued, almost concerned. They seemed all right, kind enough – especially the one with the large mustache. He could be Father Christmas's younger brother, all big and burly like that, with the rosy cheeks. The other one, the one who kept serving tea, was wiry and skinny, like an old jack rabbit.

"I'm not entirely sure as to where I am, actually," said Ben, looking around.

"Well, you're on a ship, lad, *The Queen Fredericka.*"

He was where? On a ship? *The Queen Fredericka*? But no wonder the earth seemed to be moving – he was on a ship! It probably had been out to sea for hours! How did he end up here?

"Can you tell us your name? Let's start with your name."

"What?"

"Your name, lad. Do you remember?" prompted the jack rabbit man.

"Benjamin?" he offered.

"Benjamin," the man repeated. "You don't seem so sure."

"It's Benjamin," he said again, nodding his head.

"Well, it's a pleasure to meet you, Ben," the Father Christmas man said, and he shook Ben's hand. "I'm John Holiday, and this is my colleague, Mr. William Peterson."

"Everyone calls me Whip," the jack rabbit man said. "Welcome aboard."

What was he supposed to say? Thank you? "Um…how long have we been at sea?" he ventured.

"A few good hours." The jack rabbit man, Whip, looked to Mr. Holiday for confirmation. "We've done a number of leagues."

"A number?"

"Let's put it this way, too many for you to try and swim back when they throw you overboard," Mr. Holiday said.

"Throw me overboard?!"

"Well, that's what the crew do with stowaways! Captain's orders," Mr. Holiday said, as if it was common knowledge.

94

"But I just, I mean, I didn't, how could…throw me overboard?"

Both Mr. Holiday and Whip burst out laughing.

"That was unfair, John! The poor boy's face!" Whip finally managed.

"Relax, son! Nobody's going to throw anyone overboard! They might shackle you to the mast and have you swab the deck, but not throw you overboard!"

"*Shackle me to the mast?*"

Another burst of laughter. This time Ben laughed along nervously, unsure of what was going on, and not taking his eyes off the two men.

"It's all right, son. You can relax," Mr. Holiday said, when the two men finally composed themselves. "You're perfectly safe. No one will throw you overboard, or feed you to the sharks, or anything like that. There isn't even a mast to shackle you to. We'll get you introduced to the captain and get things sorted out."

"You're not the captain?"

Mr. Holiday smiled. "No, lad, I'm not. I'm not even one of his crew, only a passenger, much like you, perhaps a bit more officially, though."

Ben was quiet.

Mr. Holiday smiled. "You're worried about the captain, aren't you? I can see it in your face."

"I am."

"It'll be fine. You've not committed the biggest of crimes,

as far as I can tell. It would be helpful if I could tell him what happened, but I'm thinking you're not remembering things too well right now. Do you remember this?" he asked, and gestured to the crate. "Do you remember getting in? Did you plan it, get in there yourself?"

Ben looked at the crate as if he were seeing it for the first time.

"If you ask me, it's a pretty risky way to travel," Mr. Holiday continued, inspecting the inside of the crate. "Especially since I don't see any food or provisions in there with you. How did you think you would get out again, seeing that it was nailed shut? Someone meeting you on the other side?"

Ben continued to stare at it, but no memories surfaced. He didn't remember how he'd gotten in there.

"I don't know," Ben answered truthfully. "I don't really remember," he began.

"No, I don't believe you do. Not yet, anyway. That looks like quite a nasty bump to the face, and I'm supposing you've maybe got more than just the bruise." Ben touched his face as if he had forgotten about it.

"Perhaps you should have a bit more tea." Mr. Holiday could see Ben was uneasy. "Run into a spot of trouble, did we, Ben?"

Something inside Ben stirred uncomfortably. Something needed to be remembered, but what?

"What do you remember?" Whip asked. "Do you know why your clothes are wet?"

At first, Ben thought that maybe he had wet himself, but no, he was damp everywhere. Yes, I was in the water, I was in the sea, Ben thought. And then, almost by instinct, Ben put his hand in his pocket to see if he had lost something and touched the key to No. 4.

Then the memories came back.

They came to him quickly, but backwards – first it was Barlow on the docks, then getting to the docks, then the train from Sugarhill, Sugarhill itself, and Mackenzie, Mr. Purchase… Mr. Holiday and Whip looked at him, noticing his expression.

"What do you remember?"

Perhaps it was the warmth of the hold. Perhaps it was the concerned way in which Mr. Holiday had asked him. Perhaps it was the fact that Ben felt safer than he had in the past two days, because once he started talking, he could not stop. With his voice echoing faintly in the hold, he told them about being left with his uncle, reading about his parents' death, and then that distressed phone call from his sister. He told them of the arrival of the first Mr. Purchase, and the apparent death of his uncle, of his imprisonment inside a tinman, and being taken to Sugarhill (and then meeting the second Mr. Purchase), and all that lead up to his eventual escape, and his hope of finding some way back to England.

The men sat in silence, listening intently as he went on and on. Ben talked so much, trying to relay as much detail as possible, that tea was brewed again to fuel the rest of the story.

His grandfather had always said that the best stories were told over a cup of tea – Ben had just never imagined that he would be the person doing the telling!

"And the last thing I remember was being back in the harbor, trying to get on this very ship. I don't know how I ended up in here though. All I remember is thinking that if he were to find me again, he would kill me."

Ben thought that perhaps Mr. Holiday and Whip didn't realize it was the end of his story because neither of them said anything when he finished.

"That's it, by the way," he said awkwardly.

Mr. Holiday was stunned. "Ben, I have to be honest here. It has to be said. That was probably the most incredible story I have ever heard a boy tell. Truth is, I was expecting to hear that you ran away from home or something, that you had gone on some kind of an adventure, you see? I am truly surprised."

After some more thought, Mr. Holiday spoke again.

"Let me just see if I've got this straight then, Ben. You're heading back to Europe because the last thing your sister said to you was that she was in trouble?"

"Yes, sir. Big trouble," he said.

"Big trouble, of course. And you're trying to go all the way to Switzerland to help her?"

"Yes, sir."

"By yourself?" Mr. Holiday confirmed.

"Yes, sir."

"Just you?"

"A one-man army?" Whip asked.

"Yes, sir." Ben wasn't feeling quite so sure anymore. "She's my sister," Ben explained, as if a reason was necessary. "She's my family, and maybe the only family I've really got right now. Don't you have a family?"

"Not as you might define yours, but yes, I do."

"Wouldn't you do that for yours?"

Mr. Holiday smiled. "I guess I would."

There was an awfully long silence. Nobody spoke. Nobody even seemed to move.

"I see," Mr. Holiday finally sighed. He stared at the floor for a few moments again and then looked at Whip, who wore an expression that said the answer to the problem was the most obvious one in the world. He sighed again. "Well, then, we had better get started," he said.

"Get started on what?" asked Ben.

"On getting trained up. It's been a while since I've had to do anything like this, and I don't intend to let a bit of personal rust get in the way of a victory," he said. "It'll be a nice little adventure."

Ben's face lit up. "You mean you're going to help me?"

"Well, I can't let a decent chap like yourself face the enemy alone!" Mr. Holiday said firmly. "My boy, if you would allow me to assist you, I would see it as a great honor."

"I might as well join you, too," said Whip.

Ben leapt off the crate and held his hand out. He didn't

wait for Mr. Holiday to take it though. He reached right out and grabbed his hand, shaking it.

"Thank you, sir! Thank you both, ever so much!"

"This deserves a toast," Mr. Holiday declared.

Ben raised his cup nervously. "Thank you. I really do thank you, and on behalf of all the Bloomswells," he began, raising the cup to his mouth.

Mr. Holiday barked a laugh as he got caught up in the moment. "The who?" he asked.

"The Bloomswells," Ben repeated, the cup poised.

"What about them?" Mr. Holiday asked, a slight furrow in his brow.

"We thank you," answered Ben a little uncertainly, the cup lowering slightly.

Mr. Holiday's face fell. "I beg your pardon?"

Ben glanced at Whip to see if he was confused as well, and he was, but he was more focused on Mr. Holiday than anything else.

"What did you say your name was?" Mr. Holiday asked Ben, his eyes boring into Ben's.

"Benjamin. Benjamin Sebastian Bloomswell."

Mr. Holiday cocked an eyebrow and continued to stare.

"Not a very common name, Bloomswell. Any relation to Jack Bloomswell?"

"He's my father," Ben said, wanting to smile, but not entirely sure if he should.

"Oh, I see." Mr. Holiday's voice was no more than a whisper.

The words hung in the air while all of the color drained from Mr. Holiday's face. The excitement and energy were gone from the room, and the three stood in silence. Ben looked between the two men, conscious of how foolish he was for trusting them so quickly and without reserve.

"Do you know him?" Ben ventured.

Mr. Holiday took the smallest of steps backwards. "You could say that."

Ben didn't know what to say. He was suddenly a whole lot more nervous than before. Perhaps he might be thrown overboard after all.

"I think that's enough excitement for tonight, don't you?" interjected Whip suddenly, breaking the silence. Ben realized he had been holding his breath. "I think it's time we all get ready for bed. Ben, let's see about getting you someplace to bunk for the night." He took Ben's cup, replaced it on the little crate and put his hands on Ben's shoulders, guiding him away. Ben looked over his shoulder and saw Mr. Holiday walking away from them, out through the door and into the darkness.

"Was it something I said?" Ben asked Whip a little while later, as Whip was making him a sort of bed. Whip didn't answer immediately.

Of course it was something you said, Ben told himself. The man had gone positively Jekyll and Hyde at the mention of his family name – especially when he told him who his father was. How could anyone not like his father? But then

Uncle Lucas's words ran through his head, and Ben considered that perhaps his father had more enemies than Mr. Purchase. Ben himself had seemingly made a whole number of enemies in the past few days alone. And how many enemies could one make in a lifetime? What were his parents *doing*?

"If I were you, I wouldn't let myself worry about it tonight. Try to get some sleep," Whip said, standing up, regarding his work. The bed wasn't much of anything, really. A folded blanket as a mattress, spread atop two wooden pallets pushed together, and another blanket on top to help keep him warm during the night. Whip had set it up in a secluded part of the hold, where Ben was less likely to be crushed by a moving crate in the middle of the night.

"Well, good night. Oh," Whip trailed off. "We might want to get you into something clean and dry first. No point in catching your death from cold when the world is out to kill you anyway."

Whip brought him a small tub of hot water, and said he would see what dry clothes he could find. Alone, Ben removed the key to No. 4 from his pocket and tucked it safely between the covers of his bed before starting to undress. It felt like he was shedding old skin – peeling away the clammy layers, unsure of finding salvageable parts underneath. He looked down at himself, feeling particularly small and scrawny, and saw that the pinch marks from the tinman were now black and yellow. The hot water felt good on his skin as he wiped it with a cloth.

When Ben heard Whip approach, he scrambled to cover himself up, but Whip only smiled and said, "You'll get over it soon enough. In confined quarters like these, there's not always a lot of privacy."

Whip gave Ben a pair of long johns and left some of his own clothes to wear in the morning, promising to help him find better fitting ones once they arrived in England. Then Whip bade him good night and walked away. Ben extinguished the small lantern and crawled in between the covers, lying there for a while listening to the alien sounds. Things were gurgling and creaking all around him, whether it was the ship itself or the crates adjusting as the ship seesawed, he didn't know. He was worried that he wouldn't get any sleep at all, but it soon overtook him, leaving him almost dead to the world.

Chapter 14

MY BOUNTY LIES OVER THE OCEAN

The sun was just about to crest on the horizon when the dark figure came to stand at the end of the now empty pier. He was amazed by how one boy consistently managed to elude him and leave such trouble in his wake. The boy obviously takes after Jack and Katherine Bloomswell more than first assumed, he thought.

Things had not worked out as he had hoped, but he found solace in the fact that, for a while, the boy was inaccessible to everyone, not just him.

Staring blankly into the distance, he knew he had to reformulate his plan, or come up with a new one. Since the boy had taken it upon himself to leave America, none of the provisions made were of any use. He would have to create similar provisions elsewhere, and quickly at that.

The question was where to create them. If England was in fact where the boy was headed, then he was in luck – England was also *his* home, and he knew how to operate there. He could make many things happen there.

For now, the next step was to get himself passage across the great Atlantic again. The boy would soon be with him.

Chapter 15

HIDE AND GO SEA

There was no birdsong to wake him the next morning, no brilliant rays of sunlight, no smell of a hearty breakfast wafting into his room from downstairs. Ben had slept so deeply that it took a while for him to come to his senses again, took a while to remember just exactly where he was and what was going on. He fumbled with the matches to light the lantern. Everything looked the same as when he'd gone to sleep. *Except for the massive knife that was pinning down one corner of his blanket.* Ben stared at it in disbelief. Had it been there all this time? Had Whip put it there to…to what? Hold the blanket down? Or had he left it there in case Ben needed to protect himself? Protect himself from what? He slowly extended his hand and touched the hilt.

"That might have been your head, you know."

Ben jerked his hand away and looked around to see who was talking.

"Pardon?" he ventured.

There was a short silence.

"That might as well have been in your head," said the voice again. Ben looked in the direction the voice had come from and strained his eyes to see. He could barely make out the figure sitting solemnly on a crate. It was Mr. Holiday. He was staring straight at Ben.

Ben realized what he had just said and looked back down at the knife. He swallowed.

"Get dressed and come next door," Mr. Holiday said, getting up. "And bring the knife. You'll need it."

When Ben heard the door close behind him, he jumped out of bed and quickly dressed. He was grateful for the suspenders Whip had left him. He had to shorten them quite a bit to keep the trousers from falling down, the trouser legs needing to be rolled up just to enable him to walk. When he had finished dressing, Ben strung the key to No. 4 on a spare bit of string and hung it safely around his neck. He had some difficulty removing the knife – it had pierced the pallet so deeply that he had to use both hands to pry it loose.

The second that Ben opened the door and smelled whatever it was that was cooking on the little stovetop, his stomach rumbled loudly. It had been empty for long enough now, and it was going to groan until it was satisfied. Whip turned from where he was busy at the stove and looked around.

"Was that what I think it was?"

Ben nodded in embarrassment.

Whip laughed. "We better get something inside you before the whole ship hears. Take a seat."

Only then did Ben see that a table had been laid with a crisp, white tablecloth and silverware. It was set for three people, and Mr. Holiday was sitting at what looked like the head of the table. He eyed Ben suspiciously as he sat down.

Ben placed the knife carefully in front of Mr. Holiday, unsure if he should say anything.

"How many doors does this room have?" Mr. Holiday asked suddenly.

"Pardon?"

"Without looking around, how many doors does this room have?"

"Doors, sir?"

"Yes, doors, Bloomswell. Doors."

"Two?"

"Is that a guess, or do you know?"

"It's a guess, sir."

"That's another thing, you're too honest. You'll have to learn the value of a good lie, young Bloomswell."

"Yes, sir."

"Two doors, then?"

"Y-Yes, sir."

"And where are they? You're wrong, by the way. But where are the two you know of?"

"There's the one behind me, and the other one is, um, is…"

"Fancy a look?"

Was he allowed to say yes?

"Have a look, Bloomswell."

Ben looked around the room and did, in fact, count two doors – there was the one he had just come in, and then another one down to his left. But if he was wrong, then where was the other one then? Would Mr. Holiday lie to him simply to make him doubt himself?

"I still only see two, sir."

"You sure?"

Mr. Holiday sighed. "Look under the table," he instructed.

Ben looked under the table and saw that the table has been placed right on top of a trapdoor.

"Oh. Three?" he ventured.

"Correct."

Then, before he could catch himself, he asked, "Did you put the table on top of it simply to test me?"

This produced a rather amused expression from Mr. Holiday. Whip turned around from the stove to look at them, a small smile on his face.

"Very well done, Bloomswell. Yes, we did. But now, can you tell me why I asked you about the doors?"

"No, sir."

"Lesson One: Never enter a room without knowing where

all of your available exits are. Doors, windows, even a crack in the wall if it's big enough, anything that helps get you away from a situation you're not in control of, see?"

"Yes, sir."

There was another moment of silence.

"Well, what's wrong?" Mr. Holiday asked.

"I'm not sure I understand, sir."

"What don't you understand? You said you needed help, didn't you? Well, I'm helping."

"But I thought that after last night, you…"

"Well, yes. About last night. I'm afraid I owe you an apology. My behavior wasn't very becoming, and I should have been more sympathetic to your situation. I apologize."

Ben never could get his part in an apology right. Was he supposed to thank somebody for apologizing, or simply accept it? And what was this urge to find something to apologize for himself? He was sure that there was probably something he had done wrong. "Thank you, sir," he said experimentally.

Mr. Holiday nodded his head, apparently satisfied.

"Would you mind if I ask you a question?" Ben asked.

"Go ahead."

"Do you *know* my father?"

Ben could see that Mr. Holiday was grinding his teeth. He sighed and nodded slowly. "Yes, you could say that. I've met him only twice though, and the first meeting took years to happen. And with all due respect, that one meeting would have been enough."

"You don't like him very much?"

"It's not a case of not liking him, lad," he said. "When you grow older, you'll realize life is not always about liking people. You can get along perfectly well with someone without necessarily liking him. It's about respect. And I respect your father. But I don't, I guess, well, you're right. I don't particularly like your father, no."

"Then why are you helping me?"

"In short, I owe your father a favor."

"You owe my father a favor?"

"Do you repeat everything that you hear?"

"Sorry, sir."

"I owe your father a favor."

"What kind of a favor?"

"Well, I would tell you, but you keep interrupting me with your incessant questions."

"Sorry, sir."

"The truth is, he indirectly saved my life some years ago, and I have been indebted to him ever since."

Ben was about to ask him what he meant by "indirectly," but caught himself just in time and remained quiet. He didn't want to risk not hearing the rest of the explanation.

Mr. Holiday eyed him knowingly and continued.

"I don't like being indebted in such a way. It robs me of a certain amount of control. Debt like that can only be repaid by a particular caliber of favor. Ask anyone that knows me, and they will tell you that men like your father and me don't take owing favors very lightly. There's an honor among men like us. And favors are a very serious business. Helping you will be repaying that favor. And we'll leave that conversation there, shall we?" It was more of an order than a question, so Ben didn't ask anything else. There was still one thing to talk about though.

"I can see it on your face, boy. Another question. What is it?"

"The knife, sir."

"The knife? Oh, the knife! Yes," he said, picking it up. "I walked straight up to you and pegged this right in next to your head last night, and you didn't even so much as stir, much less wake up. If I was one of those men that you supposedly left back in New York, you would be dead right now."

"John," Whip tried to interrupt, but he was silenced by a raised hand from Mr. Holiday.

"Now, having said that, you probably needed a good night's sleep, and in present company you're in no danger. But you'll have to trust me when I tell you, boy," he said, leaning further across the table, "the people that you've gotten yourself involved with are not going to wait for you to get your beauty rest. They don't follow anyone's curfew, and they certainly won't practice restraint when it comes to getting what they need, or getting the job done. Your nights of sleeping with both eyes shut are over. It's one eye and both ears open from now on, you understand? My advice is, get yourself a chum – a really good mate that will watch your back when you can't watch it yourself. Make sure his life depends on yours as much as yours on his."

Mr. Holiday sat back into his chair. For some reason, Ben looked past him to Whip for a second. Was Whip that chum to Mr. Holiday? Mr. Holiday smiled as if he knew what Ben was wondering.

"But be careful who you put your trust in. There are people in the world who'd betray their own mother, never mind a friend. Understand?"

"Yes, sir."

"Good. Now, for Pete's sake, what is keeping breakfast?"

"You were talking so much I didn't want to risk getting spit in the pot," Whip said. "Hold on, here it is." He put a loaf of bread and a steaming pot down between them. It smelled glorious, making Ben's stomach speak again.

"One of Marley's old standby recipes."

Ben was about to ask who Marley was, but then Whip lifted the lid. The contents gave Ben a surprise.

"Beans? You made beans?"

"Well, yes," said Whip.

"But it smells so…so…good! It smells like a roast – like potatoes and gravy, and Sunday tea!"

"I've put other stuff in there; it's not just beans. Better get used to them though, after the fresh things go off, they'll be all we have."

"If they taste as good they smell, I don't think he'll have any problem with that, Whip," said Mr. Holiday. "Here you go."

Mr. Holiday dished out a steaming portion of beans and put it down in front of Ben, handing him a spoon. Ben was very quick to dig in. His senses went into overdrive as the spoon hit his mouth – nothing else in the world mattered at that moment except for the rich aroma and the smooth spiciness. He chewed quickly, following with a bite of bread, luxuriating in the heat of the food as it slipped down his throat and into his stomach. He took a few more bites before he became aware that he was being watched. Had he forgotten to say grace? He noticed that neither of the two men were eating.

"Why aren't you eating?" he asked, his mouth still full of food.

Mr. Holiday sighed.

"We're just waiting to see how long it takes for the poison to take effect."

Did the man just say *poison*? "I beg your pardon?"

"Well, Whip thinks you'll be dead in about five minutes or so. But in my opinion, at the rate you swallowed it down, you should be dead within half of that."

"You poisoned it?" Ben looked down at the bowl in front of him. A minute ago his food was a bowl of creamy goodness that held all the promise of better things to come. Now, its dirty color and pungent aroma heralded his finality.

He looked up at Mr. Holiday beseechingly, who gave a sorry kind of smirk, and said, "Never trust anyone, my boy."

Along with his burning mouth, Ben could feel his heartbeat picking up, and soon it was racing so much he thought it might burst through his chest and explode right there in front of him on the table. He pushed the bowl away and doubled over.

"Mouth burning, is it, boy? That'll be the poison taking effect," Mr. Holiday said. "Heart racing?"

That's when Ben slumped down off his chair and onto the floor. He couldn't believe it – he was so close, he had gotten so far. How stupid could he have been? And poor Liza! What would become of her? No one would be able to rescue her! What had he done?

But time passed, and slowly but surely his mouth stopped burning, and he became aware of the clatter of silverware. He opened his eyes and stared off into space. What was going on? Did it not work, or was it simply taking it's time? Could he possibly be immune? His heart picked up its pace again, but this time for a completely different reason. If he was immune to the poison they had given him, there might still be a chance – but he had to act quickly! If they realized he wasn't dead they would surely try to kill him again. He had to escape. But how? He was on a boat in the middle of the Atlantic! How could he? Where could he go? Think, Ben! *Think!*

"Well, now you're just letting it get cold, and it'll go to waste, boy," he heard Mr. Holiday say.

Play dead, thought Ben. That's the only chance to get out alive – play dead. He tried to lie as still as possible. If only his heart would stop pounding.

"Ben, get off the floor," Mr. Holiday said.

Ben lay as still as he could.

"Ben?"

What was Mr. Holiday up to?

"Oh, please, Ben! The food wasn't poisoned. Now get up off that floor."

Ben opened his eyes.

"Ben? Did you hear me? I said the food wasn't poisoned. Now get up and eat your food before it gets too cold."

Ben sat up and peered at them from under the rim of the table.

Mr. Holiday stared at him as he continued to chew his food. "Lesson two," he stated casually, before taking a bite, "never eat food made by someone other than yourself in times of extreme danger. You never know what someone might slip into it. At the very least, have the cook eat some of the food first."

"You didn't poison the food?"

"No."

So much for being immune.

"But my heart, and the burning?"

"Chili powder," Whip said. "If we had any milk it would take it away pretty quickly."

"Your racing heart was all of your own doing. All we had to do was prompt it. The poison was all in your head, we just manipulated what we knew would happen to suit our needs. We made a mountain out of a molehill and you climbed it. And that brings me to lesson number three: Your mind is one of your most powerful and valuable weapons – don't let

anyone use it against you. You must know yourself. You'll
need to study yourself like you would anything in school.
Learn your foibles and habits, so that you may break them.
Trust me, not knowing oneself has been the downfall of many
a man. Understood?"

"Yes, sir."

"Good. Now sit down and eat."

Later, when the table had been cleared and all signs of breakfast
were packed away again, it was obvious to Ben that no time
would be wasted in preparing for what lay ahead of him. Or
rather, of *them*. He had suddenly, inexplicably, found himself
part of a team. Granted, it was a small team, but it was a team
nonetheless.

"How are you at hide-and-go-seek, Bloomswell?" Mr.
Holiday asked, as he rolled up his shirt sleeves.

"The game, sir?"

"Yes, man, the game."

"Pretty good, I think."

"Well, we'll see about that. You're about to play a lot of it."

"Sir?"

"Here's how it's going to work, Bloomswell. The fact is, I
haven't told the captain that you're on his ship," Mr. Holiday
said. "I know I said I would, and that it would be fine, but I'm
not *sure* it would be fine, so I haven't told him. That means, if
he finds you, he'll know you're a stowaway, and since Captain

Henry is an old romantic about the seas and her customs, he just might have you walk the plank, or feed you to the crew." He paused for minute. "So if I were you, I wouldn't let him find me. Now, in the spirit of fairness, if you're ever with us, doing something we need doing, and he finds you, you'll be safe. I'll do the explaining. But if you're ever not with us and he finds you, you're on your own – we don't know anything about you. And that includes when you're sleeping. Those are the rules. It's time for you to start thinking on your feet, and it's now or never. Once we touch ground in England, who knows what we will encounter. Understood?"

Ben nodded his head.

"Good."

They walked back into the hold of the ship where Whip was busy unpacking the crates.

"Why are you on board a freight ship instead of an ocean liner anyway?" Ben wanted to know.

"To be able to keep an eye on everything we're bringing back over. We wouldn't want it to fall prey to prying eyes or sticky fingers, now would we? I know many a dirty pirate that still sails these oceans. How are you coming along?" he asked Whip, who was now busy repacking the crates.

"Great. I even found something to keep me busy for a while – that new trick I wanted to work on."

"So, all of these are yours?" Ben asked, looking at the vast quantity of crates standing before him.

"Heavens, no!" answered Mr. Holiday. "Only these six

crates here are ours, including the one we found you in."

"I hope I didn't damage anything."

"No damage done, Bloomswell. Well, not by you, anyway. We hit some unexpected rough water earlier and heard something break. It turned out it was one of our show mirrors. We were inspecting our crates for more damage when we found you. Lucky for you, you were in the crate with the tent."

"The tent?" Ben looked at some of the strange and exotic things being taken out of the crates. "Are these things from a circus?"

"Yes."

"Are you from a circus?"

Mr. Holiday sighed. "I run and master a circus, yes."

"So the tent, is that the Big Top?"

"Oh, no! The Big Top would never fit into a crate that size! No, that tent is for a smaller attraction outside. The Big Top is already at home."

"But your circus, I mean, it's a real circus with elephants and acrobats and clowns and all?"

"Yes, sir!"

"And lion tamers?"

"Yes, sir!"

"How about fire-breathers?"

"Ben, we even have a Bearded Lady!"

"Really? What about a Strong Man?"

"If you ask nicely, he might just make you another cup of tea."

"You mean, Whip?" Ben looked over to him. Whip waved. "Our very own."

"But how? He's so skinny!" Ben whispered.

"I know!" Mr. Holiday laughed. "You'd think a stiff breeze would blow him over! Don't ask me how, but that man is strong. Probably the strongest man I have ever known."

Ben looked at Whip as he single-handedly pushed and pulled some of the larger crates around. He didn't seem to have a problem with any of them. It was true, looking at Whip you'd never guess that he had such a physical advantage. "What about the rest of them? Your troupe, I mean. Where are they?"

"They're all back in London already, waiting for our return."

"Wow. A circus!"

Mr. Holiday looked at Ben. "Would you like to have a better look at what we've got?"

Along with the tent there were about twenty mirrors of varying shapes and sizes, a whole box of ornamental swords, beautifully decorated juggling balls, a handful of brand new leather whips, a crate filled to the brim with various costumes of all shapes, sizes and colors, a whole crate of colorful fabrics and a large box of assorted bits of makeup. Whip was unpacking and repacking each crate to take stock. So far it had been determined that only one of the mirrors had broken during the sudden squall.

"What's this?" asked Ben, pointing to a large, domed container.

"That's Pearl's makeup."

"There sure is a lot of it."

"Well, she uses quite a bit of it each show. There are about three more of those somewhere," he said, as he referenced his list.

"Who's Pearl?"

"Pearl is our resident sword swallower and part of what might be a new acrobatic act. You'll get a chance to meet her, I hope. She's a special young lady, heart of solid gold, she has. And frankly, a person you'd want on your side in a fistfight."

Ben tried to picture a beautiful girl with a name like Pearl who got involved in fistfights.

"On the subject of fights, if we're about to deal with people that are willing to do that to an unarmed boy," Whip said, nodding at Ben's swollen eye, "we had better start preparing for a fight of our own. Ben, is there anything that you're good at, something that might be of value to you in a fight?"

"I can hold my breath underwater for a very long time."

"Well, unless you plan to swim to London, that's perfectly useless. Anything else?"

"Not really," Ben answered.

"No? Did your father not teach you anything?"

Ben shook his head.

"That's surprising. I hear he can be pretty handy with all things sharp," Mr. Holiday said.

"Oh, well, I've had a few rapier lessons with a tutor."

"That's something. Ever go up against your old dad?"

"That's more something left for my mother," Ben admitted.

"Your mother? Really? Your mother fences?"

"All the Bloomswells do. Besides, my father needed a sparring partner."

Both Mr. Holiday and Whip seemed impressed by this.

"All right, then," Whip said. "That's a good start. Grab one of those swords from the box there, and we'll see what you can do."

"Now?"

"No time like the present. Besides, we don't have much time left. Two weeks may seem like an eternity, but believe me, they'll be over sooner than you think."

Chapter 16

THREE PRAYERS

"So, tell me again exactly what it is you did," Mr. Purchase instructed Barlow, his words precise and slow.

Barlow had trouble speaking. Mr. Purchase's hands had enveloped his neck almost completely as he squeezed it. But he managed a few words, and Mr. Purchase listened.

"So you thought you'd not only allow him to escape Sugarhill, but also give him a helping hand. I see. Well, this is making perfect sense," he said, without a hint of emotion either in his voice or on his face. Barlow tried to speak again.

"Oh, you thought you'd left him for dead, did you? That the tide simply carried him away?" Mr. Purchase said, with mock interest. Barlow didn't say anything more because Mr.

Purchase had tightened his grip. "Here's what you actually did: Not only did you and my dear brother fail to secure one of our only two bargaining chips in this endeavor, but a place that is very dear to me was nearly destroyed. Then, to make matters worse, you, with clear intent, managed to allow the boy's corpse to simply drift away. Would you say that I am being accurate in my description of the events?"

Barlow nodded as well as he could. His head was throbbing, and he felt as if he were about to faint.

"Good. Now, tell me this. If you were me, how would you deal with someone like you?"

Barlow could not help but shut his eyes tightly in fear, knowing full well what Mr. Purchase would do.

Mr. Purchase smiled. "Precisely."

He gave Barlow's neck one last good squeeze. For the first time, there was a glint of malice in his eyes. Then he dropped his hands and walked back to his desk. "Consider yourself fortunate then, for having had the forethought to be helpful in the beginning," he said softly.

Barlow remained where he had fallen, gasping for air. For a few moments, the crackling fire behind Barlow was the only other sound in the office.

"Since we are moving the project away from St. Catharine's, but cannot bid her farewell just yet, we are sending a relief team to watch over the lady's wards. You are listening, aren't you?" he asked, as his white eye caught the light. Barlow, still stunned that he wasn't dead, immediately stopped coughing.

"The men are wound up and ready to go – all they need is a chaperone," he said, holding out a piece of paper for Barlow to take. "The ship departs in an hour."

It seemed that Mr. Purchase was done. Barlow did an awkward bow and made for the door.

"James," Mr. Purchase said.

Barlow turned to face him immediately.

"If I were you, I would make absolutely sure that the boy *is* dead. That he hasn't ended up on a ship somehow. And then I would pray for three things. One, for safe passage. Two, that you and my brother have the clarity and wisdom to not disappoint me again, and three, that Jack and Katherine Bloomswell never find out who was responsible for the death of their one and only son."

"Begging your pardon, sir," said Barlow in a rasp, "but I thought they were taken care of?"

"The wife is, *supposedly*, but her husband is still proving to be a problem – that is, the last time we knew where he was. But don't get too comfortable about the wife yet, James. You've seen what she is capable of, and I wouldn't put anything past her. And no matter her situation, I do believe she would be rather upset to find out that you were personally responsible for the death of her child."

Chapter 17

NEEDLE AND THREAD

Days passed, days filled with all sorts of activities, from sparring with swords and other weapons, to learning how to juggle. "If you can juggle on the high seas then you can juggle anywhere!" Whip said, as an array of objects passed from hand to hand. Training was occasionally interrupted when Captain Henry was on his way, requiring Ben to scramble for a hiding place. So far he had been lucky, tucking himself into the small shadows of the ship.

And because he wasn't under Mr. Holiday's or Whip's protection while he slept, he had to find a new spot for his bed, one that wouldn't be visible to the captain and his crew. He surveyed the hold meticulously, and soon found a good spot. It was small, but still a rather comfortable corner of the hold, blocked off from view by crates stacked one on top of another. He had studied these crates for a couple of days before making his final decision, and noted how they hadn't moved, even during the seesawing in rougher waters. In the mornings, Ben folded up the blankets and hid them, just to be extra careful. His bed was out of sight and mind, and the only way he could be found during the night was if someone knew to climb the little fort of crates and come looking for him. Since neither Mr. Holiday nor Whip knew where he was sleeping, Ben had to be extra diligent about waking up in the mornings, else run the risk of missing breakfast – even if it was just beans.

Along with Mr. Holiday, Whip tutored Ben in everything from the basics of the high wire to some elementary gymnastic maneuvers, which Ben took to remarkably quickly. And since he seemed to enjoy the gymnastics in particular, Whip let him in on the new trick he wanted to work on.

"At first I used things like cannonballs. You know, small, heavy objects. When I realized that the weight wasn't so much an issue as the size and shape of what I was throwing, I moved on to sacks of potatoes and such. But I've been thinking that a human touch might just make it a whole lot more impressive," he said, "especially when we start lighting the ring on fire!"

"Using sacks of potatoes for what?" Ben asked.

"The working title is 'The Needle and Thread,' but I think it needs work. It doesn't have the effect I was hoping for. It sounds like somebody's grandma is about to do the trick, like knit a sweater in under a minute or something."

"But what's the trick?"

"Here, I'll show you." Whip had the machinery of the trick all set up. "It's a lot like the game basketball, come to think of it. But instead of a ball, I'll have an assistant, probably a beautiful girl, Pearl probably, and instead of the basket, I'll have a flaming ring, which will also mean that whoever I throw at it will go straight through instead of being caught by it like a basket would do. I'm also thinking of making it move around to increase its impressiveness."

Ben looked at the large ring sitting in one corner. It resembled the rings that lion tamers used, and was charred and black.

"Right! Now, I'll stand right here while you move the ring to anywhere in the room. It doesn't matter where or how far, you can take it wherever you like."

Ben ran over to the ring and moved it around as Whip picked up a lumpy sack. He tossed it up in the air a couple of times, assessing its weight.

"Are you ready?" he asked Ben.

"All set!" answered Ben, backing away from the ring.

Whip turned his back and positioned the sack so that it was hanging straight down between his hands. He glanced at the ring over his left shoulder, then looked back at the sack and then at the ring again. When he was satisfied, he slowly bent his knees, keeping his eyes trained on the sack.

In one great, fluid movement, he cocked his knees and heaved the sack over his head, releasing it at the perfect moment, allowing it to soar through the air and straight through the middle of the ring. It crashed against the far wall and flopped onto the floor.

"Now just imagine," Whip exclaimed, before Ben could say anything, "that the ring is moving around the room about twenty feet off the ground. And now imagine, if you will, the ring on fire, the girl flying straight through it!"

After a moment's thought, Ben asked, "And is she going to crash into the wall as well?"

Whip regarded the sack on the floor.

"Right! Well, no, not exactly. There's still a next step. I'll show you later. But for now, the idea is that she lands dramatically, and hopefully gracefully, too. When we practice, we'll get something for her to land on, something soft."

"Oh, I see."

"And I was thinking that later on we could have multiple rings going at the same time, maybe more than one girl," he said, eyeing the ring a little more skeptically this time. "So what do you think? Is it something you would pay to see?"

"How beautiful is the girl?" asked Mr. Holiday, who had snuck in during the trick and watched it from the shadows.

"Do you really think it's something Pearl will want to try?" Whip asked eagerly.

"That girl is fearless; she'll try anything," Mr. Holiday answered. "But she'll want to know that the kinks have been worked out."

"Of course."

"I'd get it perfect before I ask her, if I were you. Practice with a more lifelike object."

Whip nodded in agreement. And then, "What do you say, Ben? Want to give it a go?"

Chapter 18

A Game of Catch

Ben convinced Whip to demonstrate the trick with a sack Ben's size, stuffed to match Ben's weight, before he agreed to help. He also insisted on putting the crash-landing mattress Whip gave him through vigorous testing.

Then, the only thing Ben had to do was to keep his body as rigid as possible.

"Pretend your body is a plank of wood instead of that lumpy bag, and I'll do the rest," Whip explained.

Mr. Holiday gladly assisted in varying the distances between Whip and the ring, and no matter where Mr. Holiday moved the ring and mattress, no matter how the ship swayed on the water, Ben always sailed straight through it and landed comfortably on the mattress.

But just when Ben thought that he and Whip had mastered the trick, there was a surprise: Mr. Holiday was to become a bigger part of the routine.

"Your turn, John," Whip said, passing Mr. Holiday the small bag of resin. "Ben can get a little slippery at times." Mr. Holiday patted his hands with the resin to make them sticky.

"What's going on?" Ben asked.

"It's the last little touch to the trick, just something to add a little pizzazz," Whip answered.

The two men looked at Ben, who was suddenly aware that he was being left out of the joke.

"What is it?" he asked nervously.

"We're just going to play a little game of catch. The same rules apply as before, Ben. Your body is a plank of wood, you just let it fly. I'm going to throw you as before, but this time, instead of landing on the mattress, John is going to catch you."

"Catch me?"

"Don't worry, he knows what he's doing. We've been practicing."

Ben looked at Mr. Holiday, who was standing ready at the far end of the room. Ben thought it was funny how he had come to trust Whip, but still wasn't completely sure about Mr. Holiday. At least on the physical side he looked strong and up to the task of catching him.

"Okay," he said, aware that his heart was racing again.

Whip smiled and gave Mr. Holiday the thumbs-up. Ben

assumed his position in front of Whip, holding his body rigid and ready.

"The important thing to remember," Whip told him, "is to be the plank until he puts you back down, okay? Oh, and be careful. Mr. Holiday can tickle."

As Ben went soaring through the air, his arms held out straight in front of him, he could see Mr. Holiday and the back wall coming closer. Mr. Holiday's eyes were trained on Ben, his hands held up ready to grab hold of him.

Ben shut his eyes as the metal wall of the hold rushed towards him, and he soon felt the grab and pinch of Mr. Holiday's hands and the chafing of his shirt against his sides. When he opened his eyes, he was held firmly above Mr. Holiday's head, the metal wall not even an inch away from the tips of his outstretched fingers.

Mr. Holiday lowered him down and inspected him. "How was that for you, lad?"

Ben's sides were still smarting, but he nodded his head and smiled. "You should try it sometime."

Mr. Holiday laughed.

"Are we going to do it again?"

"If you're up for it, lad."

"Sure, I'll just go back."

"Go back? I'll throw you back from here."

"You? You're going to throw me?"

"Uh-huh," Mr. Holiday confirmed.

"But do you know how to? I mean, do you know about

the leg and bending and all, about the height and weight thingies?"

"Easy, Bloomswell. Relax. Whip has taught me well, I think. And I promise you, I have been practicing. There are no broken potatoes on my conscience. No broken Whip, either."

"You threw Whip?"

"I've been practicing on him for a little while. You're in good hands. Besides, I'll make sure there's an extra serving of pudding for you tonight."

Knowing that Whip had been put through the trick before made Ben feel a lot more relaxed, and the added promise of extra dessert didn't hurt either. He allowed Mr. Holiday to throw him.

At first it felt different from Whip's technique, what with Mr. Holiday's larger build and bigger arms and hands. But when he was finally flipped over Mr. Holiday, it was exactly the same as when Whip threw him.

The trick was nearing completion.

There wasn't a whole lot else to do on the ship, other than eating, sleeping and practicing. Whip and Ben alternated between the newly named "Wings of Fire" and regular sparring sessions. Soon, the sparring sessions grew longer and more intense. They were also taking place all over the ship, when and wherever the two of them could fight unnoticed and uninterrupted. Whip would sometimes surprise Ben, coming at him from the shadows. He explained it was in order to keep Ben on his toes, to accustom him to being aware at all times and using his changing environment to his benefit. He was expected to fight just as well in a large open space as on a rickety staircase where there wasn't a lot of room to move, much less swing a sword.

Ben did sometimes wonder about the noise they were making, concerned about whether or not they might be heard by the captain. But he reckoned he was with Whip, and Whip would be the one doing the explaining.

Ben's favorite place on the ship was down where the engines were, where it was noisy and hot. Ben felt as if he had really earned something after a session down there.

It was after such a session that Whip and Ben sat down with Mr. Holiday, taking a break, back in the hold. Both of them were red-faced, hot from the physical exertion made worse by the pressing heat from the engines, neither of them speaking. They were exhausted.

Whip stretched his neck, running his index finger between his sweat-soaked collar and neck to help himself cool down. Mr. Holiday adjusted his own collar slightly, then suddenly he lifted his head, seeming to listen for something.

"Did you hear that?" he asked, in a tense whisper.

"What?"

"Quick, Ben! The captain! Hide!"

Ben nearly kicked over the tea cups as he scrambled to get

away. He darted behind the first crate he could find, flattening himself against it and straining his ears to listen. But instead of footsteps, he heard soft snickering. He peered around the corner of the crate and saw the two men, both bright red from trying their best not to laugh. When they saw Ben's worried expression they couldn't contain themselves any longer.

"You should have seen your face!" Mr. Holiday said, nearly falling off his seat.

Ben got out from behind the crate. "That was not funny," he said, as he retook his seat.

"Oh, it was very funny!"

And seeing the men truly enjoy themselves like that, Ben couldn't help but crack a smile himself. Perhaps it had been just a *little bit* funny.

Slowly but surely the ship crept up on England.

Home became more of a certainty, and Ben found his heart racing happily every time he allowed himself to think of it. But he was also scared of being too late to be of any good to his sister or his parents. He tried to quell those fears by working extra hard in his training sessions.

"We have a problem," Mr. Holiday said abruptly, during breakfast one morning. He had just been to see the captain about their arrival at port. Ben didn't like the tone of his voice. It held genuine concern.

"What's the matter?" asked Whip.

"Ben, when you were forcibly removed from your uncle's house, then locked up before managing to escape, only to find yourself on a ship for England…you didn't happen to do any of that with your passport, did you?"

"No, why?"

But Whip realized what Mr. Holiday was talking about. "John, surely getting Ben back into England through the shipyard won't be a problem. I mean, it's hardly a place for passengers, now is it?" he asked.

"That's what I assumed, too. But the captain has just informed me that they've really tightened security. All crews are being inspected, proper documentation required."

"But Ben's English! Surely when he opens his mouth they'll realize he belongs there?"

"We can't take that chance. Who will we say he belongs to? Why don't we have any papers for him? How will he explain getting onto the boat in the first place? As part of the act? I'm on an official warning as it is because of Keg and those explosives. And, if Ben tells them the truth, who knows what will happen to him, who will get involved? It might just get him into more trouble, and he can't afford that right now."

"How about the way he got onto the ship in the first place? We can put him back into a crate and simply take him off like that," Whip suggested.

"Then there's the problem of customs. They're inspecting

all goods, foreign and domestic, and in most cases keeping them at the dock for clearance. There's no telling how long that will be."

"Why all these strict rules all of a sudden?"

"It's all to do with the king's birthday celebration. They're taking extra precautions because of the festivities."

"But that's months away!" Ben said.

"His actual birthday, yes, but the ceremony takes place in a couple of weeks."

"How long will he be detained if he's discovered?"

"However long is too long," said Mr. Holiday.

"Liza needs me! It's already been *too long!*" Ben added.

"Well, there must be another way! If we had Keg's cannon we could have shot him into London," Whip grumbled.

Mr. Holiday suddenly froze. His right eyebrow cocked, and the corner of his mouth began to twitch. Inspiration had hit.

"I have an idea, but we might need the help of the captain and his crew."

"The captain? But then he'll know I've been here this entire time."

"Ben, the captain already knows you're here."

"Really?"

"Yes, I told him the very night we found you."

"But you said you'd changed your mind. You said he'd have me walk the plank if he ever found out! You said he'd feed me to his crew!"

"Don't get all in a huff, Bloomswell. You had to learn a new skill and thinking that the captain had the traits of a pirate helped you learn it."

"But…but…"

"Are you more upset that you were lied to, or that you were gullible enough to believe it?" Mr. Holiday asked. That shut Ben up for a second.

"Can't it be both?" he asked.

Mr. Holiday smiled.

"It most certainly may. Now, Whip, where did we pack away that harness and bodysuit?"

Chapter 19

TWO HEADS ARE BETTER THAN ONE

Night had already fallen by the time the ship docked. Ramps were lowered, and the dock workers started unloading cargo while the ship's crew readied themselves for inspection.

Mr. Holiday and Whip joined the line, passports ready, not saying a word to each other, Mr. Holiday whistling the tune to his opening act. He had put on his best cloak, combed his hair and waxed his mustache. He looked absolutely regal in comparison to the crew. Whip was all wrapped up in scarves and kept his head down, following Mr. Holiday as if on a leash.

"Passports, please," ordered the officer, as Mr. Holiday and Whip stepped into the little shed with its corrugated iron walls. Mr. Holiday handed his over, still whistling, keeping a keen eye on the officer.

"Reason for going abroad?"

"The acquisition of new talent, my boy!" Mr. Holiday's voice boomed.

"Talent? What's the nature of your business, sir?"

"Show business, my boy, show business."

The officer showed no reaction and continued to flip through the passport. "Specifically?"

"Specifically?" Holiday laughed. "The circus, lad. I own a circus!"

Again, no reaction.

"And 'Mr. Holiday,' is it?"

"Mr. Holiday."

"Well, Mr. Holiday, which holiday are you?"

Mr. Holiday cocked an eyebrow. "My boy, I'm all of them."

The officer eyed Mr. Holiday, then handed his passport back with a nod. "Next."

Whip stepped up and presented his passport.

"William Peterson. American?"

"Yes, sir."

"The reason for your visit, Mr. Peterson?"

Mr. Holiday interjected. "Why, this is the talent I was telling you about," he said, coming closer. "A fantastic new spectacle the world has yet to lay their eyes on!"

The officer raised his hand to silence him, his eyes trained on Whip.

"The night air doesn't agree with you then, Mr. Peterson? Being all wrapped up like you are. But what do you have by your neck? Or shall I say, what are you hiding?"

"My associate here is being considerate, my boy. Being considerate to the juvenile eye and mind, such as your own!"

"Let's just have a look at what you've got underneath here," said the officer, reaching for Whip.

"My boy, I beg you to prepare yourself for a sight your worst nightmare has yet to imagine."

If the officer was worried, his face didn't show it. He took hold of one end of the scarf and began to unwrap it slowly.

"Don't say I didn't warn you, boy," Mr. Holiday said, and took a step back. The nearby crew followed his example and retreated slightly. The officer noticed, and for the first time looked slightly unsure of himself.

On the second untwisting of the scarf, he could see hair and what looked like the crown of a head. And before he could fully unwrap the scarf, whatever it was snarled loudly. He jerked his hand back when a second head suddenly came out from underneath the wrapping and tried to bite him!

"Behold!" cried Holiday, "The two-headed monster!"

Whip had to turn his head away as Ben, who had been strapped on top of him in a bodysuit, snarled and bit wildly at the open air.

"What is that?" yelled the officer.

"That, my boy, is an abomination, is what that is!" yelled Holiday. "And you, yes, you," he said, pointing to the officer, "have awoken it! See how it foams at the mouth!"

Out of desperation, the officer reopened Whip's passport and looked at the picture. "But it doesn't say anything here about him having a second head!"

Mr. Holiday flung his arms over the officer's shoulder, pulling him in close. "Ah! But look at it, my boy! It's but the head of a child, not yet fully grown! It grew after the first head! I just hope it doesn't grow any more and take over the body. Heaven knows what will happen then!"

Every time the officer tried to come close enough to see where the head came out, Ben snapped at him, his eyes wide and wild.

"We're going to tame it before the king's jubilee, as per his request."

"The king *requested* this?" the officer asked, shocked.

"Personally," said Mr. Holiday proudly.

That was when Whip started singing a lullaby, stroking the side of Ben's head as he went along.

"What's he doing now?" asked the officer, in astonishment.

"Putting the beast to sleep, otherwise there's no rest for any of us tonight."

After a few moments, Ben pretended to relax and allowed his head to drop backwards in the nape of Whip's neck. But he kept his eyes focused on the officer, growling softly.

"Best let it sleep again," said Mr. Holiday, stepping forward and gently rewrapping the scarf around the two of them. They stood like that for a while, the officer still in shock.

"And the name of your circus again, sir?" he managed to ask.

"Holiday's Spectacle of Devilish Delights."

"I'll have to remember that," said the officer. "My boy has got to see this."

"Be sure to ask for your discount at the door, for being such an upstanding officer of the law."

And with that the two, well, three of them, were allowed to pass. Ben was finally back in London. Even if he was standing in it with someone else's feet.

Chapter 20

A HOME FOR A HOLIDAY

Ben followed closely as the two men led the way up the steps. Mr. Holiday gave three raps on the front door, then rang the doorbell for good measure. He glanced around and smiled at his two companions, obviously excited to be home again, but he quickly turned back to the door when no one answered it.

"Confound it! Where is everyone?" he hissed under his breath, giving three more raps on the door.

Then Ben heard an array of locks being unlocked – chains unstrung and deadbolts turned – before the door was finally opened. The light and the warmth from the inside spilled out towards them, and for a brief moment, Ben was caught up by the sensation that he was walking into the safety and familiarity of his own home.

They quickly marched inside and shut the door behind them.

"Whip, you're home!" Ben heard a woman's voice announce, as he put the bag he was carrying for Whip down. "It's good to see you safe and sound."

Ben saw the statuesque woman embrace Whip with zeal and then turn to Mr. Holiday. "And John, welcome home," she said, and gave him a kiss on both cheeks.

"Thank you, Mrs. Wuhl," replied Mr. Holiday.

Mrs. Wuhl locked eyes with Mr. Holiday, raising an eyebrow almost imperceptibly. Then, she looked over his right shoulder at Ben, lowering her hands from his shoulders.

She truly was a striking figure, almost as tall as Mr. Holiday, but she had the countenance of a kindly mother. The only thing odd about her was her full beard and mustache, elegantly groomed. Mr. Holiday and Whip had tried to prepare him for his first meeting with her, but despite that, a bearded woman was still a sight to see.

"Mrs. Wuhl, may I introduce to you, Benjamin Bloomswell."

Mrs. Wuhl extended her right hand which Ben took in his own, then he did a quick bow.

"How do you do?" Ben said.

"How do you do?" Mrs. Wuhl replied, a warm smile on her face. "It's a pleasure to meet you, Mr. Bloomswell."

She looked back at Mr. Holiday, but then did a double take as his words caught up to her.

"It *is* Bloomswell, correct?" she asked.

"Yes, mum."

"As in…?" she turned to Mr. Holiday, who nodded, but didn't say a word.

She looked back at Ben and slowly released his hand. "Mr. Holiday, might I speak to you in private for a moment? If it's not too much trouble?"

"Certainly," he said, and allowed Mrs. Wuhl to lead the way up the stairs.

Whip gave Ben a smile as if to say everything was all right. "Let's get you settled," he said, just as they heard the booming voice.

"What is that man's son doing in this house?" Mrs. Wuhl bellowed, before Mr. Holiday could close the door behind them.

Ben kept an anxious eye on the tinman tending the "welcome home" dinner. The group had congregated in the kitchen of Mr. Holiday's house, Ben brought to stand in front of the rest of Mr. Holiday's troupe as introductions were made.

Mr. Holiday introduced Keg, all squat and powerfully built, with wild, messy hair and piercing blue eyes hidden under a heavy brow; Deacon (who was the tallest of them all) with his impressive muscles and big, kind features; and

Marley, their tinman, "Our Cannon Jumper, The Fearless Man, and our resident chef. And of course, you've met our Bearded Lady. You'll get the chance to meet the rest once they return."

"The rest?" Ben asked, trying to ignore the steely look Mrs. Wuhl was giving him.

"Our acrobats, the twins, Whim and Knuckle; Jack, our assistant lion tamer; and Pearl, the sword swallower. Everybody, may I introduce you to Benjamin *Bloomswell*."

Keg gasped loudly before he could stop himself and instantly turned bright red from embarrassment as Mrs. Wuhl shot him a look. Both he and Deacon were suddenly alert, an uncertain look passing between them.

"Shall we all say hello?" Mr. Holiday said.

There was a mumbled greeting, the men clearly confused about what was going on. They obviously all knew why Mr. Holiday didn't like his father, and by the looks of it, they all shared his opinion.

"Well, this ought to be good," Ben heard Keg say, under his breath.

"You see," Mr. Holiday said, sitting down on a kitchen chair, "it's kind of like this…"

He told them Ben's story. Every now and then he looked over to Ben to make sure he had gotten the details right, which, for the most part, he had. He left out nothing. He even told them about the time he had tricked Ben into thinking the captain was approaching, which got a little laugh from everyone.

"Which brings him here, to this very house, and to all of you," he finished.

"It's a good story, Mr. Holiday. And quite a predicament, I'll give you that. But what does any of it have to do with you?" asked Keg, as Mr. Holiday finished his story. "More specifically, what does it have to do with us?"

Mr. Holiday considered his troupe for a moment.

"Well, I'm sure every single one of us in this room remembers what it's like to have your back up against a wall, without a single ally to turn to. He's in good company here," he said, looking around the room. "Each and every one of us has needed a friend at some point in our lives, were convinced that we would be done for otherwise. Not one of you can say differently. Now, this boy is alone in all of this except for his sister, who might possibly be in a worse predicament than he is. They need our help. If we turn our backs on them, we will be no better than those who put him in this position in the first place. Whip and I have committed ourselves to help this boy. We could go it alone, but like my father said, there is strength in numbers. And I would much rather know I have you at my back, protecting it."

Keg sighed.

"All right, Mr. Holiday. You make a good point. And I'm sorry for the lad, I really am," responded Keg, "but we're *circus folk*. What can we do? How do we go about helping them without jeopardizing ourselves, our 'way of life,' so to speak? We wouldn't want to get into trouble, would we? We have a public to think of. *And,* we have a contract to fulfill after all. Performance obligations, remember?"

"Well, I'm sure that it doesn't take a genius to realize that a favor done for Ben *Bloomswell* is a favor done for Jack *Bloomswell.* By doing this for Ben, by helping him, we would be helping out his father. His father would owe us," he said, with a stifled chuckle. "He's a well-connected man, and I think that he would be only too happy to assist us with any problems that might arise, any trouble we get into. Gentleman's honor, that sort of thing. After all, one good deed deserves another. What I'm trying to say is that he would be *beholden* to us, not the other way around."

There was a collective "Ah!" from the group, and the entire mood changed.

"Well, then, say no more," Keg said, a huge smile on his face.

"Well, why didn't you just say so in the first place, John?" Mrs. Wuhl snapped, and marched forward towards Ben. "Ben, it's a pleasure to have you here with us," she said, putting her arms around his shoulders. "You'll have to pardon our manners, but it's a little difficult to be as hospitable as one would like when *someone* doesn't share all of the pertinent information. You're very welcome here." Then she turned towards Mr. Holiday and whispered, "You might have mentioned that last bit upstairs."

"So, you're all in?" Mr. Holiday asked. "Babette?"

Mrs. Wuhl nodded her head.

"Deacon? Keg?"

"Absolutely, *aye*," answered Keg.

"Yes, sir," answered Deacon.

Only Marley seemed completely unaffected by the entire situation. He continued working in silence, moving between the stove and the sink.

"Right! So let's get started. Whip, we are going to need passage to Switzerland. Book tickets for yourself, Ben and me on the first available train tomorrow morning and be discrete about it. Get us as close to Liza's school as possible. Mrs. Wuhl, Ben here needs some traveling clothes – durable, protective and inconspicuous. And by that I don't mean something that will blend in with the crowd, I mean something that can blend in with the shadows – or a brick wall, if necessary. Deacon, we need to find out what's been happening at the Bloomswell residence. Is it safe for Ben to return? Can we collect some personal affects? And Keg, we need to find out about Mr. and Mrs. Bloomswell. See if anything has been found out since their disappearance. I'll go make some calls and prepare for our departure. And Marley, let me know when dinner is ready, please. I'm starving."

No questions were asked. When Mr. Holiday had finished, everyone simply got up and set about completing their assignments. Mrs. Wuhl came up to Ben with a twinkle in her eye and a great big smile on her face.

"We'd best get started, too. Let's get you measured up." Ben could smell candy on her breath. He guessed butterscotch. "Let me just grab my spectacles," she said.

She escorted Ben into her little sewing room, packed with costumes in various states of repair and completion, and quickly measured him. Then she rummaged through her stacks of cloth for suitable material, occasionally holding up a length of fabric and eyeing Ben over her shoulder until she found something that she thought might work.

"I'm afraid the next bit is boring, my dear. Why don't you go have yourself a nice hot bath? I'll leave some old things out for you to wear. And I'll call you later when I have something new for you to try on. For now, you're welcome to go," she said, dropping a great big ream of fabric down onto her table.

Ben couldn't remember the last time he had enjoyed a bath so much. He felt like he could soak in the hot water forever. The warm water and washcloth aboard the ship had only done as much as it could, never really getting Ben as clean as he would have liked. Now, in an actual bathroom, the bar of soap wouldn't even produce suds at first, he was so dirty, but after multiple scrubbings and top-ups of hot water, the soap gradually began giving off its foam. Once Ben was sure there wasn't a speck of dirt left anywhere on his body, he toweled off with a great big, fluffy towel and got dressed in the clothes Mrs. Wuhl had left for him.

He meandered down through the house, making his way back towards the kitchen while looking at the strange artifacts and memorabilia on display. Mr. Holiday's house wasn't necessarily cluttered, just packed to the brim with weird and wonderful objects, every bookshelf, cupboard, table and ledge a venerable treasure chest of knickknacks. The walls were covered with old advertisements and photos of the circus, photos of foreign places they had performed in and the various celebrities, including dignitaries and monarchs, they had met. He was particularly impressed by a poster that showed a young woman in the process of swallowing a sword. Written in big, bold letters in an arc above her was, *The Beauty, The Blade.*

So that's the famous Pearl, Ben thought. Even though he had a picture right in front of him, he found it difficult to imagine a beautiful girl like her swallowing swords. But then again, appearances can be deceiving. Take his parents, for example.

Ben found his way to the kitchen, which was empty, except for the tinman busy at the stove. Marley was clearly an older model, his casing a rosy copper color, and his face cast in an amiable grin. Ben wondered if it was possible to startle a tinman, but thought it best not find out the hard way. So, using the kitchen table as a barrier between him and the tinman, he purposefully cleared his throat to make his presence known.

The tinman showed no reaction.

"So, they all live here together, huh?" Ben asked, hoping to incite a response.

Nothing. "Um, hello?"

The tinman turned to face him. Ben was still feeling

uneasy about being so close to him.

"The troupe? They all live here, together?"

The tinman nodded his head in answer to this question.

"That's nice, all of them working and living together like this," said Ben. The tinman didn't respond. Ben swallowed. "My name's Ben, by the way," he said.

And then, in fluent sign language, the tinman greeted him and introduced himself as Marley.

"You know sign language?" Ben asked. Marley did not respond. The answer was obvious. "I had wondered about that."

Ben sat down tentatively. Satisfied that the guest of his master did not need anything else, Marley turned back to the stove.

"Have you been with Mr. Holiday for long?"

Marley turned back to Ben and signed, *All of my life*. He put his hand on his crest.

Ben wondered how long Marley was considered to have had a "life."

"Is that his *familia insignia*?" he asked, and being unsure if tinmen also considered it rude to point, half-pointed, half-gestured to Marley's crest.

Marley nodded.

"Do you know what it means?"

As Marley signed, his joints creaked quietly, a soft and almost melodious reverberation every time his hands happened to hit against his chest.

"I didn't know you understood sign language."

Ben nearly shot out of his seat when Mr. Holiday spoke.

"Sorry, my boy, I didn't mean to give you a start like that."

Ben smiled at him, embarrassed.

"It's all right."

"Where did you learn?"

"Olivander taught Liza and me."

"Impressive. But from what I know about your father, I shouldn't be surprised."

"I had no idea that that was how they all communicated."

"Oh, they don't. Marley here is an exception. Tinmen aren't really expected to answer back," he said, walking towards the stove. "By the way, how many doors–" Mr. Holiday started, but before he could finish his question, Ben interrupted him.

"Four. The one from the hallway, the doorway from upstairs, the pantry door and the one to the cellar," he said.

"Well done," Mr. Holiday replied, satisfied. "Tea?" He put the kettle on the hob as Marley took two teacups from a cupboard. He thanked Marley and sat down next to Ben while Marley put the sugar bowl down and took a small jug of milk from the icebox. Mr. Holiday glanced between him and Ben.

"There's no need to worry with Marley, Ben. He's a sweetheart. I've had Marley for years, and he has never raised so much as a finger to anyone. But I understand it might be a bit upsetting for you, after your experience with them."

"I just didn't know they could do that. Carry people around inside of them."

"Neither did I, but there you go. I guess they've made some advances. It's not a bad idea, if you think about it. If they can help people walk, people who've lost the use of their legs, perhaps? It might prove to be useful someday."

"I guess."

"Not that this should make up for it, but that tinman at your uncle's house was only doing what it was told. It would never do something like that on its own accord. At the end of the day, it was only doing what it was made for: following orders."

Yes, but it didn't have to follow them with such zeal, Ben thought. "Can they ever be told to kill someone?" he asked.

"I don't know. To my knowledge no one has ever tried. Tinmen only function with a *familia insignia* and will only fulfill the orders of a member of that family. If it was ever ordered to commit murder, it would be as if that family member himself committed that crime. Didn't your father ever explain this to you?"

"My father doesn't like them. He won't have anything to do with them," Ben said. And I am beginning to see why, he thought.

"What exactly makes them work? I mean, I know about the gears and mechanics inside but…"

"It's a trade secret. A secret kept by those who make them. But it helps if you think of them as a kind of pocket watch, something with a cross-beat escapement. With Marley's generation, you'll see that they never stop moving, there's always something that keeps going. When Marley is not busy you'll see his right index finger moving, as if he's tapping along to some song. It acts like a kind of *remontoire*, a secondary source of power when sheer momentum isn't already keeping it going. Now, if you stop the finger from tapping, for example, you'd have to start Marley up again, like rewinding a grandfather clock."

"Only with Marley's generation?"

"With the newer ones, the *remontoire* is built in, on the inside. You'd have to open it up in order to stop it completely."

"But what makes them do what they're told?"

"Your guess is as good as mine. But this isn't why I came to find you."

"Oh?"

"I've been making some calls, trying to see what there is to find out about your parents," he said. "Your father *is* an impressive man, isn't he? His accomplishments are only rivaled by your mother's, it seems. The two of them make quite the pair," he said, pouring the tea. "That said, I'm afraid that I've hit a bit of a dead end when it comes to what is going on."

"What did you find out?"

"That's just it. I couldn't find out anything. Not a thing," he stressed. "Not one of my sources had anything for me, at least nothing we didn't know already. They remember reading about their deaths in the paper, and then about their funeral in that same article you read. Nothing else since then has been reported, no advancements made. Not even my people-in-the-know know anything, and I know some clued-in people, Ben."

"Oh." Ben's heart was sinking.

"But saying that reveals a lot, my boy."

"Oh?"

"Your parents are *not* dead. Then where are they? My point is, for two people, of the caliber of your parents, to disappear without a trace, without a hint or a suggestion of what they might be involved in, why it reeks of foul play – and malicious foul play at that. Things that go a lot further than a black eye or two. And to make two people disappear like that is something only a handful of people are capable of. Only a few would have the resources. Now from what I've heard about your Mr. Purchase, he isn't someone who is skillful enough to do it, nor does he have the financial resources to, shall we say, employ anyone who is. What he did to your uncle and to Mrs. Pool seems more his style – rash, but also dumb and clunky, not slick and well thought out. In fact, when I mentioned his name to a friend of mine, he laughed. Apparently Mr. Purchase is not thought capable of being the driving force behind anything substantial like this. He's more of a henchman than a Moriarty, if I may borrow an example from Sherlock Holmes. It's also common opinion that both Messrs. Purchase ought to have been committed long ago." He paused. "Which forces me to ask if by chance you could remember anything else? Any little bit of information that you might have thought unimportant or silly, even? Anything that you might have overheard at that school, perhaps? Was anyone else mentioned?"

Ben really wanted to help, and he wracked his brain, trying to remember anything that he might have neglected to tell Mr. Holiday. Something was bugging him though. "Mr. Holiday, are you sure your friend knows who he is talking about? Sorry, I don't mean to be rude," he added quickly, "but my parents were sure Mr. Purchase was the man they were after. And it's not like them to make a big mistake like that. I mean, they might have made a mistake with his name, but…" Ben stopped. There was suddenly a warm, uncomfortable feeling in his stomach, just like the one he got when he knew he had done something wrong and was about to be reprimanded.

"What kind of mistake?" Mr. Holiday asked.

For a second Ben thought he was about to be sick. He was slowly realizing that *he* was the one who had made the mistake. "They thought his name was The Buyer, but—"

Ben stopped talking as soon as he saw Mr. Holiday's reaction to the name. His stomach turned.

"I'm sorry," he said softly, as if speaking too loudly would push him over the edge. "I just thought 'Buyer' and 'Purchase,' you know, were the same thing. I assumed they were the same man, that Mum and Dad has simply made a mistake. But they didn't, did they?"

Mr. Holiday was staring at a spot on the table. Ben could practically see the wheels turning in his head, and he didn't dare say anything else. When the stare broke, and he glanced up at Ben again, it was like he had completely forgotten that Ben had been there.

"Ben!" he exclaimed. "Sorry! My mind just wandered for a bit. How rude of me. Goodness, it looks like you've seen a ghost!" Ben had wanted to say the same thing to him a moment before.

"I assume Mr. Purchase and The Buyer are not the same person?" Ben said weakly. Mr. Holiday sighed again.

"I'm afraid not, my boy. They are two very different people – in more than just one way. To be honest, 'The Buyer' is not a name I thought I'd hear alongside all of this, but now that I have, everything is starting to make perfect sense."

"My uncle said that The Buyer is a very dangerous man."

"Oh, then you know about him?"

"My uncle told me very little. He didn't think I should know a whole lot."

"I would usually share that sentiment, but in light of what you've been through, I think the more you know, the better."

"What makes The Buyer such a dangerous person? And why is he called 'The Buyer'?"

"Mainly because nobody knows his real name – and people have perished trying to find it out. But plainly put, it's because of what he does. He buys things. Very unusual things. Aside from lost relics, rare and priceless works of art, The Buyer specializes in paying people for information. Anything from the classified shipping routes used by our Royal Navy, down to Lord So-and-So's daily routine. To him, nothing is unimportant."

"Why would he want to know what a lord does?"

"Well, just to give you an example of what can be done with certain information, The Buyer was linked to the death of the Duke of Framingham's only son. He apparently forged a love letter from the son's sweetheart to another man, whom the son then challenged to a duel. Which he lost. All accomplished by the purchase of a handwriting sample. What might have seemed to be useless information, used in a very effective way."

"But why does that make him so dangerous to all of us?"

"By buying information at what can sometimes be astronomical prices, he enables a lot of crimes to happen. The Buyer acts as a financier of sorts. Also, he often sells information to third parties, people who use it for their own gain, usually involving blackmail and so on. A secret in the wrong hands can cost a man very dearly, in more than just financial terms. And when The Buyer's prices are too high to be met, he has been known to strike a bargain. Those bargains usually include a favor, the doing of some dirty work for example. And if The Buyer were ever to call in all of the favors he is said to be owed, well, that would be a lot of bad people doing a lot of bad things."

"And is that what's happening?"

"Perhaps that is what your parents were, I mean, *are* trying to find out. One can only speculate."

"But how does this involve the two Mr. Purchases?"

"Maybe getting their hands on you was the fulfillment of a favor owed to The Buyer. If your parents are coming up against him, are possibly threatening to reveal his identity, he probably wanted to use you to force your parents to stop, threatening to hurt you if they didn't. That's my guess."

"And Liza?"

"He probably wants her for the same reason."

Ben suddenly wondered if during the three weeks he had been on *The Queen Fredericka,* The Buyer had managed to capture Liza. He mentioned his concern to Mr. Holiday.

"There is only one way to find out," Mr. Holiday said. "Since there is no one who is able to tell us, we're going to St. Catharine's to see for ourselves."

Just then, Mrs. Wuhl came into the kitchen.

"John, it's getting late. We best see if we can find a place for Ben to settle for the night. It'll be a busy day tomorrow."

"Certainly, certainly."

"I was thinking there'd be no harm in letting him bunk in one of the twins' beds."

"Oh, no need. He can sleep on the sofa."

"I thought of that, but we'll be traipsing through that room till who knows what time of the morning, and he'll not get any rest."

"Not the one in the lounge, the green one, upstairs. It's very comfortable."

"The sofa upstairs?"

"The one in the study. I've dozed off on it on a number of occasions."

"The *study*? But that's your offi–"

Mr. Holiday gave Mrs. Wuhl a look. "Yes, the one in the study will be just fine," Mr. Holiday announced.

Chapter 21

B is for Beholden

The mere thought of bed made Ben tired and groggy, and he willingly excused himself from his hosts and made his way up the stairs armed with a lantern and a set of blankets and sheets. On the first floor landing he found the door and walked towards it, noticing how loudly the floor creaked under each and every footfall. The door too, creaked loudly as he opened it. He slowly walked into the room, finding himself in a rather well-used study.

Much like the rest of the house, there were curios and knickknacks everywhere. The shelves were stuffed to the gills with books – rows upon colorful rows of them against one wall and photos and other framed pictures lining another, while piles of yellowing newspapers dotted the floor. Ben cared for none of these because there, standing proudly against a wall, was his bed. Placing the lantern on the nearby side table, he laid one sheet on top of the green sofa cushions and topped it off with another sheet before putting his collection of blankets down on top of them. Not even bothering to snuff the lantern, he stripped down to his long johns and slid in between the sheets, sighing with relief as he shut his eyes, waiting for sleep to overtake him. But it didn't.

Ben opened his eyes and stared at the ceiling. He slowly tilted his head to the right and surveyed the shelves. All of those books. Then he glanced at the desk and its piles upon piles of paperwork. He sighed. He was so tired, but he knew what he had to do. Pushing the sheets back, he swung his legs off the sofa and stood up. Where should he start?

Taking the lantern with him, he walked over to the bookshelf and inspected the books. Some looked incredibly old, while others seemed as if they'd been bound yesterday. Some were incredibly thick, and others were slim and slender, stuck in between their obese neighbors like passengers on a crowded bus.

Ben tugged a book at random, flipped it open and read a few words. It was a history of chess. A history of the origins of the game, its internationally famous players and their most famous matches. It appeared to have been read quite a lot, if Ben was any judge of the ear-marked pages, the worn spine and notes in the margins. Who knew Mr. Holiday was such a fan of chess?

Ben tried to find the book's original spot on the shelf, but it had already disappeared, taken by the other books, desperate for more space for themselves. He chose a random spot and used all of his might to squeeze the book in. He reached for another book, but changed his mind when he saw the title, *Aesop's Fables*. He knew that one.

Then he saw five large books, like photo albums, sitting next to one another one shelf above him. He pulled on the fourth one, and had to act quickly as it seemed to fling itself from the shelf. He caught it before it fell to floor, surprised at how much heavier it was than it looked. He looked at the door and waited a few moments before taking the book back to the sofa.

Paper crinkled. It was a photo album, but instead of holding photographs, it held newspaper articles, each one telling of a person or event of some sinister persuasion. There were articles about theft, articles about arson, murder and fraud, about crime ranging from the petty to more grand and severe, and where each article mentioned a possible suspect or proven culprit, Mr. Holiday had written notes, giving his own opinions about whether or not he thought them to be true.

Where there was no name mentioned, where either the authorities had been at a loss or the reporter had not yet been made privy to the information, Mr. Holiday had come up with his own suspects. On more than a few occasions, there was written only one name, apparently when Mr. Holiday was sure of who it was.

Lady Auster von Hame Robbed at Royal Opera House by Costumed Renegade read one article, with the name "Pagliacci" written in red ink above it.

Taxi Cab Driver Found Slain in Continuing 'Vampire Slayings' read another, the name "The Porcupine" in Mr. Holiday's writing above that, and so on. It was rare for an article not to have a name written above it. But when Mr. Holiday seemed to be at a loss, question marks riddled the page.

Then Ben noticed something interesting about the volume as he flipped through the pages. It seemed to have been organized in a specific manner, each article alphabetical by suspect or perpetrator's name. The albums had been organized in order, and the current volume covered M through Q.

Ben looked back up at the remaining volumes and wondered if a Bloomswell, or more specifically, his father, had ever made an appearance. He shut the M-Q book and replaced it on the shelf, swapping it for the first volume. It was equally as heavy, but this time Ben was prepared.

Back on the sofa he opened the book at random. He was immediately aware of one big difference between this book and the last. Where the previous book's articles were about the questions surrounding the crimes, about the criminals evading the authorities and proper justice, this one was more about justice being done, about crimes being solved and criminals captured.

Police Apprehend 'The Canary' at Tower Bridge Showdown, One Officer Killed and above it, the name, "The Beholden," written in red ink.

McTreer Twins Arrested and Charged in Kensington Theft Syndicate, and again, "The Beholden."

Arrests Made in Paddington Fire Drama. Police Claim Case Closed, and "The Beholden."

Where there was the occasional article about an unsolved or new crime, it was followed by a later article, the crime having been solved, the criminal tracked down and arrested.

In each article, whenever a mention was made of the crime being solved by an unknown constable, a leading detective or a contracted specialist, it was always circled with a red pen and corrected to "The Beholden." Ben figured The Beholden to be a real-life version of Sherlock Holmes, a venerable crime solver. Why hadn't he heard of him before? Surely if he was this good, he would have heard his name mentioned, wouldn't he?

Impressed as he was with this real-life hero, he flipped through the pages in search of his family's name. No results. It was probably a good thing, especially after what his uncle had said.

He replaced the album on the shelf and sat down behind Mr. Holiday's desk, surveying the vast mess on top of it. More articles, freshly cut out and awaiting organization in the appropriate albums lay on one pile, while a collection of maps were bundled together on another. There were more books, and a stack of unframed photographs. How Mr. Holiday got any work done at this desk was a mystery!

It was simply because the telegrams were lying closest to him that he picked one up and read it:

CEASE CELEBRATIONS RE BEHOLDEN IMMEDIATELY STOP CONNIVING BLOOMSWELL ALIVE AND WELL STOP WILL INVESTIGATE STOP it read, and was signed by someone by the name of Farden. Ben's heart immediately picked up its tempo. He brought the telegram closer to him and reread it quickly. He seemed to finally be getting somewhere! He picked up the next telegram. This one read differently, obviously having been sent before the first one.

CONGRATULATIONS ON DEATH OF CONNIVING BEHOLDEN STOP GREAT REASON FOR CELEBRATION STOP MUST LET ME KNOW HOW YOU DID IT STOP FARDEN

He noticed the one similarity between the two telegrams: "conniving" Beholden and "conniving" Bloomswell. Could it be? Suddenly, it was like the earth tilted, throwing Ben's mind off kilter and into a swirling whirlpool. Was The Beholden his father? Was that it? He thought back to the articles he had just read. No wonder he didn't find *any* articles regarding his father. He had found *all* of them! Could it be true? The album had been full of articles! And all of them suspected by Mr. Holiday to be linked to The Beholden. His father!

He looked at the first telegram. It was dated a few days after the newspaper article telling of his parents' death. The second telegram was more recent, dated only a few days ago. At least that gave him some hope. If The Beholden was his father, then at least he had been "alive and well" just recently.

However... *You must let me know how you did it*, the telegram read. This unnerved Ben most. Had Mr. Holiday been the one who'd tried to kill his father?

Suddenly, his seemingly gracious host was no longer the affable and kind gentleman from their journey across the Atlantic, but had turned back into the bully he had met the first morning, the one who pretended to poison food and such. Ben had been suckered into believing that he was among friends, that he was safe and secure! And now he was in this villain's office, of all places. How foolish could he have been? No wonder Mr. Holiday didn't want him to sleep in someone else's bed. He probably wanted to get him alone. Maybe take care of him in his private room, where no one else probably dared set foot.

But why then had he not killed him while on *The Queen Fredericka*? Surely that would have been much easier than bringing him all the way back to England and to his house. No one had known that he was onboard.

There were so many questions, one leading to the next, and what made it more confusing is that he could think of both positive and negative answers for each one! And it didn't help that he was so, so tired!

With his mind already reeling, Ben considered his options. What was he to do now? Make a run for it? Perhaps climb down from the windows behind him and maybe… what? Go back to No. 4? Or stay and run the risk of meeting his untimely demise during the night? How far down was the ground, anyway? If only someone like Sherlock Holmes were here to ask for advice… Ben sprang to his feet as he felt the heavy touch of Mr. Holiday's hand on his shoulder.

Chapter 22

Too Old for Adventure?

Ben blinked his eyes furiously. The bright morning sunshine was streaming in through the windows he had considered escaping through just a few moments ago. He looked at Mr. Holiday in surprise. Why hadn't he heard him coming in? All those creaking floorboards! The creaking door! What had happened? Then realization dawned. He had fallen asleep in Mr. Holiday's chair! There was no denying what he had done, especially since he still had the telegram in his hand.

"Deacon's back," was all that Mr. Holiday said, almost excitedly. "He's in the kitchen and has some news I believe you'll really want to hear. And breakfast's ready," he finished, making for the door. Ben glanced down at the telegram and imagined what it must look like, him sleeping in Mr. Holiday's chair, among his private things.

"Mr. Holiday," he began. "I'm sorry, I'm, you see, I…" he tried to explain.

But Mr. Holiday looked at him, bewildered.

"I haven't the faintest idea what you're talking about, my boy," he said. Then he walked off, the floorboards creaking loudly.

Ben returned the telegram to the desk, trying to smooth out some of its creases. Then he quickly dressed, before running downstairs to the kitchen, to find the entire household waiting for him.

"The house is dark and locked up, there's not a soul there. But it's being watched, all right. And whoever it is isn't making himself very inconspicuous. There he was, clear as day, leaning up against a lamp pole," Deacon told them.

"What about Olivander. Any sign of him?"

"Who?"

"The family butler," Mr. Holiday answered.

"Butler? None of the neighboring staff knows anything about a family butler, I'm afraid. I heard tell of a cook, and had a gardener talk to me about one or two maids he had taken a fancy to, but no butler."

Ben's heart sank a little. Not only were his parents gone, but now Olivander was missing, too. It seemed to never end!

"He would have been a *big* help," Ben said quietly. "We could really have used someone like him right now."

"Sounds like we can use all the help we can get," said Mrs. Wuhl.

"That reminds me, Babette, we'll need to send a wire to Pearl. I'm afraid time with her mother and sisters must be cut short. We'll need her here when we get back."

"Yes, John."

"So that settles it. The house is not an option right now," Mr. Holiday said, as Whip entered the kitchen with a triumphant air.

"Ta-dah!" he exclaimed with a beaming smile, slapping the train tickets down on the kitchen table.

"What'd I miss?" he asked.

"Ben can fill you in as you pack," answered Mr. Holiday.

"I'm sure it doesn't do much for your spirits, does it?" said Whip, after Ben had told him all that they had learned from Deacon.

Ben shook his head as he attempted to fold and pack one of the outfits from Mrs. Wuhl.

"I guess it never occurred to me that Olivander would be anywhere but waiting for us at home. But now, thinking about it, it would be the last thing he would do – sit there, waiting. He probably left the day he read the article about my parents." Ben caught himself and tried to clarify. "I don't mean *left*, but left to help."

Whip smiled at him. "I know."

And then Ben thought of something. "Whip, do you think Olivander might have gone to America when he found out about my mum and dad?"

"He might have, I guess. If he's the type of man you say he is. But you're more likely to have the answer than me, Ben. You know the man."

Ben wracked his brain. He remembered that the newspaper was British, so Olivander probably found out about it long before he did. But then he wondered if it was possible that Olivander was involved in some way. Perhaps he was in on the whole setup! After all, his father did trust him implicitly. Did he know what was going on? Was he possibly even causing what was going on? And if he was, where was he? Oh, this was so confusing!

"Easy there," Whip said, putting his hand on Ben's shoulder. "It looks as if your head is about to explode."

Ben sighed and sat down on the bed, then flew up immediately. "Ow!"

Whip tossed back the corner of the bedding to reveal what Ben had sat on. "I was wondering what happened to this."

"That's a baseball bat, isn't it?"

"It sure is! It used to belong to my dad. Kind of pretty, isn't it?" he said, holding it up to the light, admiring it.

"Are you bringing it along?"

"Yes. I doubt we'll have time for a game on this trip, but you never know when it might come in handy." Whip handed it to Ben for a look, and Ben rubbed his hand over the smooth grain of the bat.

"Like it, do you?"

"It reminds me of Olivander."

"Does he like baseball?"

"Something like that, yes."

"Probably more of a cricket man?"

For some reason that made Ben think about Mackenzie, back at Sugarhill, and he wondered if he had liked playing baseball, too. Just then, Mr. Holiday called them back down to the kitchen for some urgent news. When they got there, Keg was still trying to catch his breath.

"You won't believe what I just found out!" he said, between gulps of air. "There was a break-in at the dock warehouse last night. Apparently some thieves broke in and opened every single crate from *The Queen Fredericka*, including all of ours. They left quite a mess. But the strange thing is, nothing was taken."

"Where'd you find that out?" Whip asked.

"One of the lads who stood guard there last night told me. Apparently they had a great view of everything."

"Well, didn't they do anything about it?"

"They reported it when they could, but that was only a couple of hours ago."

"Why so late?" Mrs. Wuhl asked.

"Apparently they were slightly impeded in doing so any earlier by the tinmen that had them trapped."

"Did they see who was controlling them?" Mr. Holiday asked.

"All the lad said was that it was an American, medium-build, with brown hair. Nothing special, apparently," Keg said. Ben froze. Mr. Holiday looked at Ben, and Ben nodded. It sounded like Barlow.

"They said he seemed quite upset when he left, like he didn't get what he had come for. Some of the stuff in those crates could make a man a lot of money if sold. Not the type of things a greedy man would simply leave behind."

"Any other crates opened?" Mr. Holiday asked.

"Nah, just the ones from *The Queen*."

"Including the ones with our name plastered all over them?"

"Those would be the ones, yes."

"So they must suspect that you were on the boat, Ben. But how?" Mr. Holiday asked.

Ben shrugged his shoulders.

"They might only suspect he'd gotten on board and are just being thorough," Mrs. Wuhl offered. "It sounds like they think they've hit a dead end. Then again, if they start asking the crew questions, bribing them for information, it won't be long before they learn of Whip and you. And thanks to your little publicity clause, it might only be a matter of time before there's a knock on the door."

"Publicity clause?" Ben asked.

"I'll tell you later, boy. First things first. We have to get you on that train and out of England again, the sooner the better."

"But Waterloo station is such a public place. How do we

get him on a train without being noticed?" Deacon asked.

"You think they'll be watching the station?" Mrs. Wuhl asked.

"We have to consider it. We're back in his hometown. This is where it all started," Mr. Holiday said.

"How about some makeup then?" Mrs. Wuhl suggested.

"Whatever will make you feel better, Ms. Babette. I'd prefer a cup of tea myself," Keg remarked.

"No, as a disguise for Ben, of course," she said.

"That's an idea," Mr. Holiday said.

"We could always hide him in something again," Whip offered.

"Oh, not another box, please!" pleaded Ben.

Between being kept inside a tinman, the narrow flues of Sugarhill, and the crate, Ben had had his fill of confined spaces.

"Sorry, buddy. I forgot."

Mr. Holiday looked at Ben, eyeing him as if he were measuring him. "Well, we'll need some kind of disguise," Mr. Holiday said. "Nothing elaborate, something ordinary that would slip by unnoticed."

The troupe waited in silence as he thought, never taking his eyes off Ben. Then, suddenly, "Makeup it is. Babette, we'll require your help and the aid of your vanity case. And, if I might raid the costume department again, please."

Under the guidance of Mrs. Wuhl, Mr. Holiday emerged

victorious from the costume department (a collection of trunks containing years' worth of old show costumes) with a gray wig, a pair of shoes, a dress and a veiled hat. Once Ben had put everything on, they sat him down on a kitchen chair and set to work.

There was a lot of activity around Ben's face.

Mrs. Wuhl had armed herself with a bottle of spirit gum and a set of face paints. As she started to apply the base coat of makeup, Deacon fixed the wig to Ben's head, and once it was secure, combed its long gray hair and began twisting and tucking it into a tight bun with a handful of pins.

"How do you know how to do all this?" Ben asked.

"We all help each other in the circus, dear. We pick things up from one another," Mrs. Wuhl said, taking a firm grip on Ben's jaw and turning his face in various directions. She was slowly transforming him from the young man he was into the old woman he was to leave the country as. Occasionally she gave him instructions to squeeze his eyes shut or pucker his lips, while all the while the rest of the troupe stood behind her in silence, riveted by what they were seeing. Finally, Mrs. Wuhl let go of his jaw. She eyed Ben suspiciously. Then, giving her right thumb a swift lick, she wiped it under Ben's left eye and sat back in her chair, folding her arms across her chest. Her work was done.

There was a collective intake of breath from the troupe as they saw the full effect. Ben searched their faces for any indication of how he looked.

"Well?" he asked.

"Crikey," said Deacon, still staring at him.

"Bloomin' marvelous. He looks like my Gran' Ethel," said Keg, squinting to get a better look.

"Babette, you are a master," said Mr. Holiday.

"Why, thank you, John," she said proudly. "I do say, it is pretty good, isn't it?"

Ben got up from his chair and looked at himself in the mirror.

"You look…you look…" Whip began.

"Stupid," said Ben, unimpressed. He stared down at the dress, fanning it out to get a better look. Then he scratched his neck where the starched collar grated against his skin. He sighed. "Why couldn't I have been an old man? Why an old lady?"

"The further from the truth, the better, my boy. Besides, we had the dress handy," said Mr. Holiday.

"Oh, I almost forgot!" said Mrs. Wuhl, as she came up behind him and hung a string of pearls around his neck. "Perfect – the finishing touch," she said.

Ben's scowl was *almost* completely hidden by the makeup. As he turned to face the troupe he made eye contact with Whip, causing Whip to burst out laughing.

"It's not funny," Ben said.

That's when Keg and Deacon started laughing, too. Mrs. Wuhl shook her head in disapproval, but soon had to hide her own smile. Even Mr. Holiday had started chuckling.

"See! It's not working! You all think it's funny!"

"It's only funny because of your face right now, Ben! It looks like a monkey's bottom!" Keg said, wiping tears from his eyes.

"Don't you listen to them, Ben," said Mrs. Wuhl. "You look wonderful! You're a proper granny. Now, where'd you put your knitting?" She couldn't even finish the sentence before she started laughing, holding onto Ben for support as she bent over in merriment. Ben just shook his head, adamant that he wouldn't give in. But he couldn't stop it – he could feel the laughter come up inside him, his cheeks twitching as it did. It was when Mrs. Wuhl started running out of breath that he finally cracked a sheepish smile, making everyone laugh even harder.

"It's really not funny!" he said again, as Mrs. Wuhl sat down in a chair, clutching at her aching sides.

"I think it's time we prepare for our departure. Whip?" Mr. Holiday said, to Ben's great relief. "Oh, and Babette, I would like for you and Keg to accompany Ben to the station, please."

Later, during the last few preparations for their trip, Mr. Holiday looked at Ben with a critical eye.

"We need to see if the disguise works," said Mr. Holiday. "We can't simply have you walk out of the house without being sure that people will buy your disguise. Perhaps we can go for a walk around the square and see. Ah, but there isn't much time," he said, as he inspected his pocket watch. "Maybe if we hurry. We'll simply have to," he said, and ushered Ben into the parlor, grabbing his coat and hat. Just then, there was a knock on the door. Mr. Holiday tensed up ever so slightly and regarded Ben, wondering if he should send him upstairs and out of sight or not. He walked closer to the door, and asked, "Who is it?"

"Post Office, sir. I've a telegram."

"Oh, perfect!" Mr. Holiday whispered to Ben. "Ben, you answer the door. It'll be our little trial run," he said, and pushed Ben towards the front door.

Ben didn't know how to behave and was suddenly quite overcome with stage fright. With an encouraging prompt from Mr. Holiday, he reluctantly put his hand on the doorknob and turned it.

"Good morning, mum," said the young man, with a tip of his hat, as the door swung open. "I've a telegram for a Mr. John Holiday. He in?" he asked, his accent a thick cockney.

Ben looked over his shoulder into the house, seemingly unsure. The young man stared at him, the slightest irritated scowl flashing across his face.

"Um, I'm his mother?" Ben said eventually, his voice an affected croak.

"Oh, that's all right then," the young man said, eager to get on with his day. "Just sign here for me, and I can be on my way."

Ben took the pen and scribbled illegibly on the form he was handed, swapping the form for the telegram. He gave a small sigh of relief. It had worked! But the young man didn't leave. He seemed to be waiting for something. He cleared his throat and held out his hand.

Ben looked at it, but there was nothing in it. Then, from behind the door, Mr. Holiday stuck out his own hand and passed a coin to Ben.

"Oh," he said, and passed it on, dropping it into the young man's open palm. The young man looked down at the copper coin, then glanced into the house, a look of confusion on his face.

"Ta'!" he said, slowly and carefully making his way back down the stairs, almost afraid to turn his back on the house.

Ben was pulled back into the house, and as the front door slammed shut, Mr. Holiday shook Ben's hand.

"Oh, that was perfect. Just perfect. Well done, lad! Well done," he said, dropping the telegram onto the hall table. "He didn't suspect a thing! Brilliant! Now to collect our travel documents and the last few things, and we will be on our way," he said, making his way up the stairs and leaving Ben all alone in the parlor.

Ben sighed with relief and turned, catching his reflection in the hall mirror. He looked at himself. He had to admit, Mrs. Wuhl had done an incredible job – the little lines puckering around his mouth, the soft crows' feet around the eyes…

Then he glanced down at the telegram. Mr. Holiday had forgotten all about it. Ben wondered if it was another one from that man Farden, with news about his father. He had to know!

He stared at it for a while before glancing around the room to see if anyone else was close by. Then he grabbed it and shoved it into the folds of his dress, quickly making his way into the downstairs lavatory.

Locking the door behind him, he tore off the edges and unfolded the telegram.

BEHOLDEN FOUND IN CAIRO STOP TRICKY SITUATION STOP ASSURED OF BENEFITS BY GIVING DEATH HELPFUL HAND AS DISCUSSED STOP ADVISE STOP FARDEN

All of his fears came rushing back, and his heart was racing for two completely different reasons. He was excited and nervous at the same time. Not only was his father alive, but Ben now also knew where he was – Egypt! But, the man that Ben had placed his trust in would apparently not only celebrate his father's death, but would gladly assist in causing it – and had maybe already attempted to bring it about! What was he to do? Could he still trust and depend on Mr. Holiday to help him get to Liza?

Just then he heard Whip call his name. He folded the telegram into a tight little square and stuffed it into his undershirt. He would read it again later.

"Everything all right, Benny-boy?" asked Whip, as Ben came out of the lavatory. "You seem a bit troubled. You're not really upset about the costume, are you?"

"No, I'm just anxious to get to Liza, is all," Ben answered, making to walk away.

"Hold on," Whip said, and put his hand on Ben's shoulder, pulling him back.

"We'll get you to her, Ben. By tomorrow night, if I have my way, you two will be back together."

"I know, but still," he said, keeping his eyes averted from Whip.

"You're not alone in this anymore, Ben. We're here to help."

Ben had to catch himself before he snorted in disdain. But Whip could sense what Ben was trying not to give away, and he pressed on.

"You can trust us, we're here to help. Don't you believe that?"

For the first time, their eyes met, and Ben said, "I guess I just don't know why you're helping me – especially with Mr. Holiday not liking my father. No one here seems to, and they've made that very clear."

Whip sighed. "John and your father have had, shall we say, a *complicated* history. A number of people in this household have. But we're not talking about him, right now. We're talking about you. And I promise you, you can trust Mr. Holiday and every single one of us."

"But what complicated history? Why won't he tell me? It's not like I can ask my father about it, can I?"

"John will tell you when the time is right. Until then, you're safe with him. I trust him. I trust him implicitly. And I would like for you to trust me. I will help you, Ben. *We* will help you. I give you my word."

Ben looked at Whip. He seemed completely honest and

sincere. Ben could tell that he meant what he said, and it helped. At least there was one person he felt he could trust, even if Mr. Holiday seemed to have ulterior motives.

"Okay?" Whip asked.

Ben nodded.

"Okay, then. Come on, Mr. Holiday is waiting for us in the cab."

Chapter 23

THERE WAS AN OLD LADY
WHO WAS AN OLD LIE

Ben spotted the massive poster on the station wall even before they pulled up to the curb. There was no mistake. The picture was too detailed and accurate for that. It was Mr. Holiday, larger than life, a top hat in one hand and a rolled up whip in the other, proudly standing underneath the bright and bold letters. *Holiday's Spectacle of Devilish Delights.* "Subtle," commented Mrs. Wuhl dryly, as she looked to see what Ben was staring at. "It's been there for ages. And they're all over the city."

"Of all of us," remarked Keg. "It's horrible."

"Oh, please. I've seen how happy you are when someone asks you for your autograph," she said, and unlatched the taxi door.

With the veil pulled down over his face, Ben was helped from the taxicab by Keg, and they stood together outside Waterloo station. He had been briefed on how to act in public during the cab ride over, but he still felt silly waiting for help down the couple of steps when he could have just jumped them. But so far, the trick seemed to be working. Although there were people everywhere, no one had shown any particular interest in the little old lady and her two companions. As soon as the wheelchair they had brought along was set ready for him, Ben sat down in it and waited as Keg draped the knee blanket over his lap.

Ben wasn't sure whether it was because people paid respect to the wheelchair, or whether it was because of their pace, but people got out of the way as the three of them barreled down the platform.

Mrs. Wuhl, carpetbag clutched firmly in her right hand, umbrella in the left, lead the way as they made a beeline for their train, Keg steering the wheelchair expertly behind her.

She had tied a wide scarf around her face, hiding every trace of her beard and mustache, and as such, she was able to move through safe from stares, looks and pointed fingers. She had temporarily deserted the personality of the Bearded Lady, and suddenly adopted a new character, as if by the flick of a switch. There was an air of importance about her, and people were responding to it.

She handed Ben's ticket to the first attendant she came across and followed him as he led them to their train. When they came to his compartment, the attendant unlocked the door and secured the bag on the baggage racks. Then he helped Ben out of the wheelchair. Ben feigned a struggle as best he could as he climbed into the compartment.

As the attendant turned to Mrs. Wuhl, he noticed that she was still holding on to her bag. He assumed she also meant to board the train and reached out to take it. But his hand stopped dead a few inches from its handle. Mrs. Wuhl had given him a look. It was the type of look that made you want to crawl down a deep hole and stay there for a very long time.

Where it was rumored that Helen of Troy's beauty launched a thousand ships, Babette Wuhl's arched eyebrow moored them again in turn.

The attendant slowly pulled back his hand, scared to move. He did not dare break eye contact with her. "Begging your pardon, mum," he said, giving her an awkward smile, unsure if it was the right thing to do.

"Shut the door and leave us," she said.

The attendant quickly did a half-bow, half-curtsey towards Mrs. Wuhl and scampered away.

"Be safe, my dear," Mrs. Wuhl said to Ben, through the open window. "I'll make sure Marley has the tea ready when you all return. Look after each other, and Ben, you bring that sister of yours back safely now, you hear?"

"Yes, mum."

In the distance they heard the conductor shout, "All aboard!" and a blast of steam shot out from under the locomotive.

"I'd better be off. Keg?"

Keg gave a quick nod of acknowledgment to Mrs. Wuhl and another one to Ben as a goodbye, then disappeared back into the main station, off to get Mrs. Wuhl and himself a cab back home.

"But what about Mr. Holiday and Whip? Aren't they coming?" Ben asked, a little nervously.

"They said they'd meet up with you soon. It's safer this way, not to be seen all together. But no worries, right?" Mrs. Wuhl give him a conspiratorial wink. Ben nodded.

"Safe journey, dear," she said, and walked away.

Ben pulled the window back up, lowered the rolling blind and locked the door. Outside, the shriek of the departure whistle sounded, and Ben's heart leapt. Were Mr. Holiday and Whip even on the train? Had Mrs. Wuhl meant they would meet up with him "soon" on the journey, or "soon" as he arrived in Switzerland? He wasn't expected to make the train journey all by himself, was he? Especially not dressed as a wizened old woman?

As the train lurched forward, clouds of steam and smoke billowed across the platform. Ben ventured a look through the window, but there was no sign of either of them. He even searched in vain for Mrs. Wuhl, but she had already disappeared into the crowds.

The train steadily picked up speed and soon was out and away from the station, it too disappearing in the distance.

Ben couldn't ignore the pang of sadness in his chest. After

all, the last time he had taken this trip he was still with his parents. They were still the two people they had always been. Everything was normal. They had all been happy, and he had been so excited about the wonderful trip to America that lay ahead of him.

A good twenty minutes later there was a knock on the door. Ben held his breath and stared in shock. Should he answer?

"Grandmamma?" asked a male voice softly. Ben heard Whip chuckle, and he realized the voice was Mr. Holiday's. Ben quickly unlocked the door.

"All right, my boy?" asked Mr. Holiday, as he stepped inside.

"Oh, you can take that veil off now, I think. Keep it close, but take it off. Once we're in France, I think you should be able to get out of the rest of that get-up," said Whip.

"Where have you been?" asked Ben indignantly. "I was worried sick that you had missed the train!"

"Oh, I'm sorry, Ben. We wanted to be extra careful. We didn't want to make anyone suspicious by getting too close to you too quickly, just in case we were being followed. But we were on the train with plenty of time to spare, don't you worry," said Whip.

Ben was angry at himself for getting so worked up about something so silly. And what made him feel worse was being dressed up like he was. He missed his clothes, and he missed his family. He sat back down, taking care not to crush his hat.

"So what do we do now?" he asked.

"Well, now we wait," answered Mr. Holiday. "First we wait to get to Dover to take the ferry, and once we're in Calais, we'll be on our way to Zurich. From there we'll take the train to Heimweh, where we'll be met by our man, who will take us to St. Catharine's. We should be there by tomorrow afternoon."

The cab carrying Mrs. Wuhl and Keg pulled up to Mr. Holiday's house. Mrs. Wuhl accepted Keg's hand as she stepped down out of the cab and marched off into the house, leaving Keg to pay the driver. As he watched her disappear into the house, he gave a big sigh of relief and felt himself relax for the first time since leaving that morning. They were home again, and had managed to get there without incident.

It wasn't that he disliked Mrs. Wuhl in some way. On the contrary, he had always felt a special kind of bond with her. She filled the "favorite aunt" role in the troupe, someone who always had a piece of candy for you. Truth be known, she held a special spot in everyone's hearts and was always up for a good laugh. Still, in Keg's opinion, when she was out and about with that bag of hers, things tended to get a little sticky. Before wishing the driver a good night, he gave him an extra big tip, as if to share his good fortune of a smooth morning. The driver tipped his hat in thanks and drove off.

Mrs. Wuhl, accustomed to the fact that there were no

servants other than Marley to help with the "tasks that ran a civilized house," made quick work of putting her coat in the front closet and sailed up the stairs with her bag clutched under her arm, eager to take off the rest of her traveling gear.

Time was of the essence, she kept reminding herself. She had plenty to do in preparation for Mr. Holiday's return in a few days. This young boy and his troublesome family. She found herself amused by the fact that she still couldn't help but snort in disdain when she thought of Jack Bloomswell, no matter what Mr. Holiday said. She reached the first landing and was about to head up to her private apartment on the next floor when a gust of wind caught both her skirt and her attention. She turned and saw the door to Mr. Holiday's study open a crack, and she could feel the cold air coming from it. Who would leave a window open, she thought, at this time of year? She pushed open the study door quickly and quietly, and when she saw the window open wide, its curtains swaying in the autumnal breeze, she didn't look at anything else, just marched into the room to shut it.

That's when she brushed up against something tall and imposing. She seemed to recognize it at first. What is one of my mannequins doing here?

But then it moved.

It turned its dark face towards her and looked at her as if it had been waiting, just for her.

Mrs. Wuhl was by no means a woman faint of heart. She had held her own against the worst of them. But sometimes…

She clutched her bag to her chest and screamed a scream that rattled the china in the kitchen cupboards two floors below.

"And then it just flew out the window!" she cried later in the kitchen, amidst a flurry of activity as Keg, Deacon and Marley scrambled to make a much needed cup of tea.

Deacon and Keg had charged up the stairs at the sound of Mrs. Wuhl's scream and had found her, white as a sheet, but alone and unharmed, in Mr. Holiday's study. She had her eyes, wide and unblinking, trained on the open window.

"It flew out the window?" Keg asked in awe.

"Yes!" she almost shouted, grabbing his hand and squeezing it.

"Incredible! It actually flew!" he said.

"Oh, Keg!" Mrs. Wuhl snapped, and pushed his hand away. "It's a figure of speech! It didn't literally fly, it leapt! Jumped straight out of that window as if it could fly." She gave a big sigh. "Are you sure there was nothing down on the ground, Deacon? Did you look everywhere? Who knows where it could have fallen."

"Yes, mum, I'm sure," he answered, gingerly placing the hot cup of tea down in front of her.

"Heaven only knows what happened to it," she said, staring off into the distance.

"What do you think it was looking for?" Keg asked.

"I'm not sure it was looking for anything!" answered Mrs.

Wuhl. "It was just standing there. For all we know, it would still be standing up there had I not come across it."

"You mean, like Marley does sometimes?"

"Exactly!"

Keg shivered. "I don't know about you lot, but sometimes he still gives me the heebie-jeebies."

"And you're sure it wasn't a tinman, mum?" Deacon asked, as delicately as he could.

"There is no chance that that thing was made out of metal."

"Shall we go have a look to see if anything is missing?" Keg asked.

"I told you, it wasn't looking for anythi–" Mrs. Wuhl began, but stopped, suddenly deep in thought. "However…"

"However, what?" Keg asked.

"The boy's blanket."

"What about it?"

"It was holding the boy's blanket. The one he slept under."

"Ben's?"

Mrs. Wuhl nodded. "Yes. It was holding it with both hands, then dropped it when it jumped out the window."

"Do you think it was cold?" Keg asked, before a quick jab in the arm from Deacon. Mrs. Wuhl didn't seem to have heard.

"It's after the boy," she said, a few moments later. "It came looking for the boy."

For the few hours it took to get there, Ben drifted in and out of sleep, waking up to a different landscape outside his window every time. The complicated clouds and gray hues of the London sky effortlessly segued into a seemingly endless expanse of ocean air as they approached the cliffs of Dover.

Whip had timed their trip perfectly. There was a ferry scheduled to depart about half an hour after their arrival in Dover, and before he knew it, the three of them were sailing along smooth waters. In Calais however, their timing was less fortuitous. The train that would take them all the way across the border and into Switzerland was scheduled to depart later in the afternoon, so Ben had to endure more time in disguise.

"We wouldn't want people to start wondering what happened to our female companion, now would we?" Whip explained. "To suddenly have a little boy in her stead might make people wonder. Don't worry, we'll get you out of that get-up soon enough. We won't have to worry about that in Zurich, there will be far too many people at the station for anyone to notice a missing little lady."

When they finally boarded the train, it felt as if they were riding straight into the night as it fell, for when it started it came quickly and severely, turning the horizon pitch black. And with the White Cliffs of Dover soon far behind them and no sign of Switzerland up ahead, it felt to Ben as if they were riding into oblivion.

Mr. Holiday was fast asleep, perched in the corner opposite him. Whip was busy juggling. He caught Ben's eye and smiled. "If you can juggle on a train, you can juggle anywhere," he said, without breaking stride.

"We might even get snow soon," said Mr. Holiday later, when he saw Ben looking out the window again. "I reckon you'd be a lot more comfortable in some of your own clothes for bedtime. You can get out of those clothes now, if you wish. But keep them handy. Oh, and sleep with the veil close at hand, just in case."

"I'll get us some dinner," Whip offered, and left the compartment.

Ben eagerly stripped off his old-woman costume and put on the new clothes that Mrs. Wuhl had made him. They felt great.

"Apparently, you and Keg are almost the same size, so Mrs. Wuhl altered some of his show clothes, some things he used to shoot out of the cannon in," Mr. Holiday said. "Her biggest job was removing all of the sequins and glitter."

The clothes were dark, the trousers slim and well-fitting, and the leather, military-like jacket fit like a glove. Ben noticed that all of the buttons and clasps were hidden in folds of cloth.

"It's to help advance the momentum you get when you're shot out of a cannon, to make the exit from the cannon as smooth as possible. Not that I see you shooting from a cannon anytime soon."

Ben admired himself in the window reflection. He

thought he looked older than he did before. Perhaps he *was* more mature than he'd been three weeks ago, before all of this had happened. *Three weeks ago*. It had felt like ages and then again, like nothing at all.

Just then, there was a knock at the door, startling Ben. Recognizing the coded rhythm, Mr. Holiday unlocked it and slid it open. Whip had returned with dinner.

"Who's hungry?" he said, passing out roast beef sandwiches.

"Where's the horseradish sauce?" asked Mr. Holiday.

"What? Is there none in the box? The fellow said he would put it in there."

"Well, not in mine. Ben, yours?"

"Not in mine either, but I prefer it as is, thanks," he said.

"Then you start, Ben. No need to wait for us."

"The dining car was packed. Everyone must be in there right now, so no wonder the man forgot. But hold on," Whip said with a sigh. "I'll get the sauce." And he was off again.

Mr. Holiday sat patiently, his sandwich splayed open on his lap, as Ben continued to eat.

When the door opened again, Whip stepped inside quickly, and Mr. Holiday clapped his hands together and smacked his lips. "All right, let's have it!"

Whip handed the small dish over, but he looked troubled.

"What's the matter?" Mr. Holiday asked.

"There is a rather surly looking tinman with a Fair Face on the train."

"What's a 'Fair Face'?" Ben asked, his mouth still full of food, his appetite suddenly gone.

"A mask designed for tinmen, to help them blend in more when they're out and about. They don't work though. You can still spot them a mile away," answered Mr. Holiday.

"But this was a custom mask. It was good. I almost didn't notice it," Whip interrupted.

"Nowadays they're only worn when people don't want their tinmen recognized, when recognition could mean trouble," Mr. Holiday finished.

"The thing is," Whip said, "I don't think it's alone."

Ben swallowed his food with difficulty.

Whip looked at Mr. Holiday, who had one eyebrow raised. Something was obviously wrong.

"Did it see you?" Mr. Holiday asked.

"I'm not sure, I couldn't tell. You never know with those things, do you? Especially not with that Face on."

"Did it react to you?"

"Not that I could tell."

"Ben, just to be on the safe side, let's have you put on your costume again," Mr. Holiday said, and Ben's throat felt as if it had dropped right into his stomach. "There's a nightgown in my bag, put that on. But put it on over those clothes. Whip, can you get this place ready for bed? I'm going for a walk."

As Ben got dressed, Whip unlatched and lowered the bunk bed from the wall. He'd nearly finished when there was a knock on the door. Whip straightened up. There had been no secret knock this time. Whoever was on the other side of the door was not Mr. Holiday.

"Get into bed and pull the veil down over your face," Whip whispered to Ben, who did as he was told. His heart was racing so fast he was sure Whip could hear it.

Whip glanced over to Ben to make sure he was ready and then slid the door open.

Chapter 24

THE WILD STEEL STALLION

"Oh, my apologies," the man said, his eyes darting around inside the compartment. "Wrong compartment."

"It's quite all right," Whip responded.

"Goodnight," the man said. He walked away, looking from the compartment numbers on the doors to the scrap of paper in his hand.

Whip slid the door shut and gave a huge sigh of relief. But Ben had had to do everything in his power not to react when he'd seen the man standing in the doorway.

"That was Barlow!" he hissed.

For a second, Whip had no idea what Ben was talking about. "What?"

"That was him, Barlow! The man in America who took me! The one who gave me the, the, oh, what'd you call it – the shiner!"

Whip looked at the door as if Barlow was still standing there.

"Are you sure?"

As if he'd ever forget that face!

There was another knock on the door, and this time even Ben recognized the secret rhythm. Whip unlocked the door for Mr. Holiday, but stopped him before he could step inside. "We have company. Ben's American friend dropped by, but didn't stay."

"Which way did he go?" Mr. Holiday asked. Whip motioned his head to the left, and without saying another word, Mr. Holiday walked off in the same direction.

Paying particular attention to the sounds coming from each compartment, he came to the end of their carriage and stepped through the noisy gangway into the next one. He'd just entered the carriage, the door behind him sliding shut, when he heard the door ahead of him open and shut as well. He picked up his pace, trying to make as little sound as possible. The painted sign on the next door he came to read *Authorized Personnel Only*. But the American had gone this way, and so would he. Besides, a sign like that had never stopped him before.

Mr. Holiday stepped across the gangway and, ruse at the ready, slowly opened the next door. The car seemed pitch black at first. He closed the door behind him. He stood still for a few moments, waiting for his eyes to grow accustomed to the darkness, then gingerly took one step forward.

"Why is it so dark in here?" he asked, faking the slight slur of someone who'd had a little bit too much to drink.

As if in answer, a figure seemed to appear right in front of him, blocking his way. As big as he was, Mr. Holiday yelped in shock, then, remembering his character, started to laugh.

"Mate, you gave me such a fright!" He chuckled heartily and reached out to the figure as if to steady himself. "I nearly wet meself!" He touched the figure's chest. He continued chuckling, just in case the tinman wasn't alone, but he also straightened up, to better see what was going on.

What he saw sent an involuntary chill down his spine. There, among the trunks and suitcases, was not just one more tinman, but at least twenty, standing in two rows, one behind the other. They reminded him of dominoes ready to topple. Or a pack of dogs, waiting to pounce.

"You all belong to anyone here?" he asked, slowly making his way past them to the door when he didn't get an answer. He reached out to take hold of the door handle, but it moved all by itself, and the door opened towards him. He gave another yelp of surprise as this time he came face to face with a real person.

"Mate! You scared me half to death, you did!" he hollered.

"Can I help you?" asked Barlow icily.

Mr. Holiday recognized the crisp, American accent. "Just

looking for a loo, mate!"

Even though it was dark, and his face was covered by the shadows, Mr. Holiday could feel Barlow peering at him.

"Sorry, sir, there's no 'loo' here. This is a private carriage, and I'm going to have to ask you to be on your way."

"Oh, yeah, of course. Sorry, my mistake. No harm meant," he replied, lifting an imaginary hat in salute.

Heading back to the door, Mr. Holiday knew full well that Barlow was looking at him. Unfortunately, he only realized he was making a mistake as he was doing it, and he wasn't able to stop himself in time. As he opened the door, light from the next carriage fell on his face, and Barlow instantly recognized him from his poster.

Barlow whipped out a pistol. Mr. Holiday bolted through the door before he could pull the trigger. He gave the handle a quick, hard tug, breaking it off out of the lock, hoping to buy himself a few more seconds in which to warn Whip and Ben. He sprinted down the next carriage, the sound of breaking glass behind him. Skidding to a halt in front of their door, he knocked frantically, but before Whip could even answer, he shouted, "He's figured out we're involved! Get the boy off the train, now!"

"Here we go," said Whip, as Mr. Holiday ran off. A few moments later, Barlow ran past the compartment as well.

Whip peeked into the corridor, and seeing it empty, he instructed Ben to get out of bed and follow him. He led him in the opposite direction from Mr. Holiday and Barlow, but his plans were thwarted when he looked through the carriage doors and saw tinmen heading towards them.

Whip stepped onto the gangway between the two adjoining cars, and without warning, took hold of the collar of Ben's nightgown, ripped it off and flung it away. Then, he jumped up to catch hold of the ledge, pulling himself up onto the roof of the carriage. When he was safely on top, he reached down, offering his hand to Ben. The instant Ben took it, he heaved him up.

It was freezing up there, the icy wind pushing at them with incredible force. But, for now at least, the tinmen were unaware of their presence above them. When the coast was clear, Whip led the way down to the gangway again. He slid the door open and stepped inside, engulfed by the carriage's silence, then led Ben along the corridor. Behind him a compartment door slid open quickly, and Ben was pulled back. Whip turned to see what was happening and saw Barlow, a malevolent smile on his face, and Ben struggling in his grip. Four tinmen came out of the compartment behind him.

"I thought your grandmother was looking a little peaked, so I went to check on her. Imagine my disappointment when she wasn't there," Barlow chuckled. "It's a funny thing really, us having the same travel plans." He turned his head towards Ben.

Ben knew exactly what was about to happen when Barlow lifted him into the air. Oh, not again, he thought.

"And as for how you will redeem me," Barlow began, but before he could finish his sentence, Ben brought his right knee up, hard. It connected with Barlow's jaw with a satisfying crack, and Barlow released him so that Ben floundered backwards against the tinmen. He was tempted to give Barlow an extra kick, but Whip pulled him away and pushed him behind him, further along the corridor.

"To the roof! Wait for me there," Whip whispered, as he turned to face Barlow and his tinmen. Ben raced down the corridor to the next gangway. He looked through the door's small window and saw more tinmen in the next carriage. Then he spotted the ladder running up to the roof of the carriage, and once again made his way up into the cold night air.

"So who are you supposed to be? The Strong Man? You look nothing like your poster. You must've paid the artist handsomely. All those added muscles? Life hardly does it justice," Barlow said, taking a step towards Whip as he massaged his aching jaw. "Now, listen," he continued, "I don't have a problem breaking something as pathetic as you, but there's hardly any merit in it with the lads. So consider this your lucky day and go back to bed." His voice was filled with venom.

Whip did not move.

Barlow sighed theatrically. "Remove him," he instructed the tinmen. "Then tear him apart."

The tinmen sprang into action, pushing past Barlow and advancing on Whip in single file. Whip allowed the first tinman to get close to him, watching as it stuck its hand out to take hold of his face, but when its hand was a mere fraction away, Whip deftly knocked it away with his left arm, and in one smooth movement, pulled his baseball bat from under his coat.

He lopped the tinman's head off with one graceful swing, kicking the disabled body away from him, hurtling it against the others. As the next tinman toppled under the weight of the first, Whip jumped over the mounting pile, his bat flying.

Seeing what Whip was capable of, Barlow scurried into the first available compartment and pulled something from his pocket, yelling into it, "We have a situation! Activate the spark units!"

In the meantime, Whip had finished with the tinmen and turned to go after Barlow.

He slid the door to the compartment open. Barlow pushed himself up against the opposite wall, against the outside door of the compartment, to try and put as much distance between himself and Whip as possible. He remembered his pistol, but he had only just drawn it when Whip neatly hit it out of his hand. Barlow glared at him, a twisted smile on his face.

"What are you going to do now, fella? Huh? Hit me? Want to fight?" he said, and raised his fists in scorn.

But Whip's attention was drawn to what he saw through

the window. Tinmen were clambering and crawling around on the outside of the train!

Barlow glanced behind him, saw them and laughed. "You can't possibly stop them all, you know. And you'll want to be extra careful where you hit these ones. You wouldn't want the entire train to blow up!"

Whip realized he needed to get to Ben and Mr. Holiday. And as the realization hit, he dropped his bat and shoved Barlow. He shoved him so hard that he crashed right through the outer door, taking a piece of the siding with him as he plummeted into the darkness. Whip heard his scream fading away. Snow had started falling.

Satisfied that Barlow was gone, Whip exited the compartment and ran down towards the baggage car. He nearly ran into Mr. Holiday, who had come running from the opposite direction. He had a sword drawn, ready for another fight.

"Where is Ben?" he said.

Suddenly, a tinman came up behind him and lunged at them. Whip stepped aside, twisted his arm around its neck and snapped off its head. Then, in one swift motion, he ripped open its chest.

"Oh, my." Mr. Holiday froze. "That's new."

The tinman's insides were jam-packed with explosives.

"They're going to blow up the train? But they'll kill Ben in the process!"

"I think that's the point!" said Whip.

"But I thought they needed him?"

"Looks like they've changed their minds!"

Mr. Holiday and Whip rushed to get up onto the roof of the carriage where they were instantly set upon by a handful of tinmen. But the two of them fought well together and quickly overcame the onslaught, only to then notice more tinmen dotted around the roof. These tinmen were passive, some standing perfectly still as the train rocked underneath them, others lying down with their arms and legs sprawled out, having latched themselves onto the roof like spiders.

"Where's Ben?" Mr. Holiday yelled.

Whip, who had spotted him first, pointed towards the front of the train. Mr. Holiday squinted against the falling snow and could only very faintly make out what he assumed was Ben, holding onto the edge of the next carriage. Something was peculiar. He blinked a few times. What was going on? Was the snow playing tricks on his mind, or was the train getting longer?

Then he saw the gap between the two train carriages getting bigger. "Whip! The train!"

"What?"

"The train! The swine have unhitched the cars!"

Mr. Holiday suddenly grabbed Whip by his jacket, bringing his ear close to his mouth so he could be heard. "It's up to you now! You have to get Ben off the train!"

"Me? What about you? I'm not leaving you!"

"Don't argue!"

The gap between the two carriages was getting much bigger.

"Do you trust me?" Mr. Holiday yelled.

Whip looked him straight in the eyes, saw the urgency there, and nodded. "I trust you."

Mr. Holiday smiled. "It's 'Wings of Fire' time."

It all happened so quickly.

Mr. Holiday bent his legs and placed both his hands around Whip's waist. He then lifted his right foot, placed it above Whip's middle, and paused. It seemed very quiet for a moment. Mr. Holiday glanced around, his eyes darting between the retreating train and their own carriage, which was steadily slowing down. His mind was going furiously, working out the height, distance and the trajectory required. And when he looked back at Whip, he was smiling. Right before he broke eye contact, he winked at him. "Get the boy back to his family."

And that was it. Balanced on his left leg, he bent further down, pushing his body backwards with his right foot extending up against Whip, his arms lifting him by his torso. It was like he'd flipped a bag of feathers into the air.

As Whip moved out of his grip, Mr. Holiday continued to roll over himself into a full somersault. Whip went soaring through the air, his arms outstretched ready for the target, like he had taught and trained Ben.

Whip found Ben lying face down on the roof of what was

now the last carriage. He reached out and Ben shot up in defense. He stared at Whip in disbelief and then noticed the distance between the carriages.

"How did you…I mean, how…?"

Whip turned around to look at Mr. Holiday, barely able to distinguish him among the tinmen. He quickly scanned the skyline, and to his utter relief, he saw the faint lights of civilization, perhaps even Zurich itself, in the distance. "We're nearly there!" he yelled at Ben. "But if the train stops, we're going to get off and run for it, okay?" Ben nodded. Whip turned back to the uncoupled car for one last look.

At that exact moment, the sky was lit up by a thunderous explosion. Ben and Whip stared at the flaming ball of fire leaping up into the white sky between the train cars. Breathless and helpless, Whip ran forward, but they were too far away to see anything.

Seconds later, the train's brakes started screaming as it slowed down. Ben followed Whip as he climbed back down into the safety of the train. They were sheltered once more, taking brief sanctuary in their old compartment.

"Grab your bag, we've got to go," said Whip.

"What about Mr. Holiday?"

"He wants us to go on," Whip said, collecting their things, trying to ignore the twinge in his heart as he handled Mr. Holiday's belongings.

"Who is The Beholden?" Ben suddenly blurted. Whip stopped what he was doing and stood upright, facing Ben.

"Where'd you hear that name?" he asked.

"Who is he? Is he my father?" Ben insisted.

"Ben."

"Is he?" Ben demanded.

"Yes, he is."

"Why is Mr. Holiday trying to kill him?"

"Whatever gave you that impression?"

Ben took out the telegram, unfolded it and handed it to Whip.

"There were more just like it in Mr. Holiday's office. One congratulated Mr. Holiday on my father's death, making it seem that he had done it himself. Had he? I mean, did he try?"

"No."

"How can I be sure?"

Whip looked at Ben. Perhaps it was because his own heart was in turmoil that he wanted so badly to reassure him.

"John was not trying, nor did he ever try, to kill your father. It's something I can't explain now, but if your father was out of the picture, so to speak, John *and* the rest of our troupe would have regained a certain kind of freedom in their lives, a freedom they didn't have under the constraints of the circus."

"I don't understand."

Whip tried to come up with another way to explain it to Ben.

"They are *beholden* to your father for their jobs at the circus."

"What does that mean?"

"It means, he is the reason they are all in the circus. They have him to thank, in a way."

"If they have him to thank, then why would they want him dead?"

"The circus, being a lesser of two evils, is still an evil, no matter how you look at it."

"The lesser of two evils compared to what?"

"I can't go into that now, we haven't the time."

"Please!"

"Let's just say to some it is a job they don't feel like doing, and your father is making sure they do it."

"Work in a *circus*? That's absurd. That's just silly. What aren't you telling me?"

"Ben."

"I need to know. Please."

Whip sighed.

"John is – *was* – a criminal, Ben. He was a thief, and a very good one. He was known as The Collector, 'collecting' priceless jewels and works of art, expensive little knickknacks, whatever he could lay his hands on. But he got greedy and he got sloppy, and he would have been the first to admit he got too big for his britches. Your father was the man who stopped him, who brought him to justice. And at the end of the day, the two of them made a deal. Your father offered him two options: prison and everything that it involved, or a kind of 'publicity clause' in which the authorities had to know where he was at all times. John chose the latter and through a rather roundabout way, ended up with the circus – not only as its master, but also as a chaperone to its troupe, a band of criminals all under the same restrictions as he was. John always remained very secretive about their arrangement, and all he ever said about it was that failure to comply would have dire consequences. Regardless, the point that I'm trying to make is, John would never really have harmed your father. And I think you know that. Deep down, by everything that you know about John, from everything that he's done for you, you know that he wouldn't harm him, much less you."

"What about the telegrams?" he asked.

"Did you ever wonder why they were simply lying about in the room he insisted you sleep in?"

"No."

"He meant for it to happen. He wanted you to find them, to read what they said."

"But why?"

"Perhaps to tell you more about what is going on. To show you a bigger picture, to give you answers to questions you didn't know needed asking. And perhaps it was a way of showing you that you can really trust him. He showed you that he had two options, and he chose this one, the one to help you."

Ben took a deep breath.

"Okay."

"Okay?"

"I believe you."

"Good. Now what we concentrate on is helping your sister. Come on, we really must get going."

Whip opened the compartment door and tossed his and Mr. Holiday's bags onto the ground just as the conductor was announcing that they were stopping to investigate what had happened. As the train gave one final jerk, Whip and Ben jumped from their compartment into the snow.

They would make the rest of the journey to Zurich on foot.

They arrived in Zurich much later than their scheduled time and more than slightly worn out after their trek along the snow-covered train tracks. Seeing the bustling station, however, gave them a renewed sense of purpose and helped them to forget their tired feet.

The station was filled with policemen, and Whip knew exactly what they were doing there. An investigation into what had happened to their train had already begun, and Whip was glad they had made a run for it. Had they stayed on the train they would certainly have been detained for questioning.

He skillfully maneuvered their way through the throng of police, enabling them to make the train to Heimweh. Ben, with a relatively makeup-free face, followed Whip mindlessly, sorrow lying in his stomach like a stone. He felt personally responsible. Both his and Whip's minds were clouded with the morning's sad events, even as they focused on their goal: reaching St. Catharine's in time.

Chapter 25

A Wake-up Call

The dark figure had crouched down in the snow to watch the smoldering carcasses of the two train carriages. He was trying to prepare himself for what would happen if he found the remains of a young boy. How much would be lost, if not everything? And how would he explain to his employers that he had not reached his target in time? How would he explain to them that he had failed? How would he explain it to himself?

He stood up and made his way down through the trees. He noticed one with a partial tinman's head rammed into its trunk. The severed wires were still sparking sporadically as they moved in the cool breeze.

So that's how they did it, he thought. They're getting quite vicious.

Later, after he had found what was left of the few human passengers and convinced himself that no part of them had ever belonged to the boy, he tried to put his mind at ease, all the time appreciating just how narrow the boy's (and subsequently his own) escape had been. This was a wake-up call for him, one which he resented needing. He knew that he would have to step it up a notch.

Luckily for him though, there could be no mistake as to where the boy was heading.

Chapter 26

CHRISTMAS IS MY
FAVORITE HOLIDAY

Whip and Ben could see St. Catharine's peeking out through the mountains as soon as they stepped off the train. Ben didn't know what he'd expected. Bolts of lightning or ominous storm clouds hovering overhead? But from the distance, everything looked fine.

"You should see her during Christmas," said an elderly man behind them.

"I would like that. Christmas is my favorite holiday," Whip replied, finishing the coded sentence.

The man nodded in confirmation and introduced himself as Peter, their guide. "I thought there was to be three of you," he said, his voice rough. "Where is John?"

"He has been detained," Whip said. "We are to continue without him. I hope that doesn't cause any problems."

"No, there will just be more room in the wagon. Now come, we must hurry, deliveries are to be made."

St. Catharine's School for Girls had been a derelict castle before its conversion to the prestigious school. This meant that there were architectural precautions in place, built to withstand enemy attacks or penetration, making entry to the school, other than through the main gates or via the sky, nearly impossible. In Ben's opinion, the school still looked more like an impenetrable fortress than anything else, its walls cupping it in a protective embrace as it loomed over the valley below.

Ben was slightly taken aback when he learned that he and Whip were to hide in gunnysacks and ride into St. Catharine's on the back of the wagon, disguised as part of the coal delivery. In theory this sounded good, but the gunnysacks seemed too flimsy to protect them from anything, and it seemed an obvious place to hide.

"But it's too obvious, ja?" Peter said, with a knowing smile. "The most obvious place to hide is often the last place to look."

Ben hoped he was right.

They made themselves as comfortable as possible among the sacks of coal on the back of the wagon, then Peter arranged more bags of coal around them and drove them up to the gates of St. Catharine's. The gunnysacks did hide them from plain sight, but they couldn't prevent Ben and Whip from getting covered in soot.

Never in his life had Ben been this dirty, this frequently.

Peter brought the wagon to a stop at the gates and waited to be let in. The tinman that stood directly behind the gates was almost as gray as the dusk surrounding it, and it was only visible by the light of its lantern, reflecting off its metallic skin.

There was a moment of tension when the groundsman came towards the wagon. He did not ask for permission before he jumped up into the seat alongside Peter and glanced back at the cargo. "I will drive with you," he told Peter in German. "I need to unlock the door for you."

Neither of the two men said anything as the wagon wobbled up the hill. As it came to a halt, the groundsman jumped off and unlocked the iron gate, telling Peter to get the job done quickly and to leave the same way he'd come.

Peter didn't argue.

While the groundsman walked back down the hill, Peter backed the wagon up into the wide doors of the coal room adjoining the castle. Once it was inside he gave Whip the signal that it was safe to get off the cart. Whip and Ben helped him unload his sacks of coal and quietly thanked him for his help.

"You'd best find a place to hide for the night. A storm is coming. Snow, too," Peter warned. "I will see you when you return." Then he bid them good luck and goodnight.

A while after Peter left, Ben and Whip heard the large metal gates of the main entrance shut behind the rattling wagon. They did as Peter instructed; they lay low and waited for the groundsman to lock the coal room door. They didn't have to wait long. The heavy bolt soon slid across the outside of the door again, the locks fastening

So, now what? Ben felt like asking. They'd come all this way to get locked up in a coal room and freeze to death?

But Whip had already found another door built into the side of the school, and he was busy picking the lock. He fiddled around inside the dust-ridden keyhole and soon produced a satisfying click. Whip opened the door a crack and peeked past it to find a dark, stone staircase leading upwards. Closing the door silently behind them, he and Ben crept up the stairs, finally inside the school.

The next door they came to was locked as well, dim light coming in through the keyhole. Whip could spy what looked like a kitchen on the other side, which luckily for them, was empty. After another quick trick with his tools, they snuck inside.

The kitchen didn't look unused exactly – it looked under-used, like only a small part of it was regularly put to use. Even the fire had been left, forgotten and smoldering.

"Where do we begin?" Whip asked Ben, figuring him to know where Liza would be. Ben didn't have a clue where to look for her. He had never been to St. Catharine's before, and Liza never talked about the layout of the school in her letters.

Not wanting to disappoint Whip, he noticed a door on the far side of the kitchen and pointed to it. "That should lead further into the school, I guess."

Whip happened to put his eye to the keyhole just as a key was inserted from the other side. They scrambled for cover – Whip behind the bulky butcher's block, and Ben inside a large cupboard. When the door opened, Ben saw a young girl walk in, carrying a large, empty bucket. She was followed by a woman, tall and austere, wearing what appeared to be part of a nun's habit. She wore only the robe, not the headdress. And behind her, in well-oiled silence, came a tinman.

Ben grimaced. He had had enough of tinmen to last him a lifetime.

The woman thrust a set of keys toward the girl, glowering at her until she took them.

"Be quick about it," instructed the woman, her accent English.

The girl hurried to the door leading down to the coal room and inserted a key in the lock. Whip cursed himself for not locking the door again, but the girl did not seem to notice anything amiss, and after a quick jingle of the keys, she opened the door and disappeared down the steps with her bucket.

They could hear her filling the bucket with coal and then struggling to carry the full bucket back up the steps. She didn't even have time to catch her breath before the woman handed her the tinman's bucket and ordered her back down the stairs again. It took some effort and time, but she managed to bring the tinman's bucket up. Then she followed the woman and tinman out of the kitchen, half-dragging, half-carrying her bucket of coal. The kitchen door locked behind them.

Whip emerged from his hiding spot first, sneaking to the door to spy through the keyhole again as Ben came out from his cupboard. Whip barely managed to catch a peek of them disappearing down the hall outside the door.

"That tinman could have easily carried both those buckets!" Ben said. "Why have her carry it?"

"Things are definitely not right here," Whip said. "The sooner we get Liza out of here the better."

They went the same way that Whip had seen the girl and her chaperones go, then down a stone staircase that led them towards another heavy door at the end of the hall. Before they could get too close to it, the door opened and the girl emerged again, her hands now dirty, but empty of the bucket. Only the tinman followed her this time, the woman remaining to shout orders from the other side of the door.

"Lock them up for the night, and when you have checked on the one in the vault, return here."

The tinman acknowledged the woman's order with a quick nod of his head and led the girl back down the corridor, past Ben and Whip, hiding in the inky shadows.

Making sure the coast was clear, they followed the girl and the tinman up the massive stone staircase that spiraled into the heights of the castle. But the silent steps eventually gave way to creaking wooden floorboards, and Ben and Whip would be heard if they followed. They had no choice but to hide one floor below, to wait for the tinman to make his way back downstairs like he had been instructed. Whip reasoned that as long as there were no other tinmen upstairs, and the others remained far down below, squeaky floorboards would cause no danger.

After the tinman left, the two of them made their way up the stairs. There was more than one door to choose from, with no indication as to which one had recently been used. And there was no telling who or what lay behind those doors.

Ben peeked through the keyholes to see if he could see his sister, but the rooms were either completely empty, or so packed with girls that he couldn't make out one from the other. And every time he crept up to look, the girls heard his footsteps and stared at the door to see who was about to come in.

Ben nearly fell backwards when at the last door somebody suddenly started talking to him.

"Go upstairs," a girl said.

Ben moved closer to the door and whispered, "What?"

"Go upstairs, we will come to get you."

"Is Liza in there?" he asked.

"Go upstairs," she insisted. "And hurry."

Ben glanced over to Whip, who nodded at him, and the two of them ran up the stairs.

The next floor up was even darker than the one before; the

one circular window in the far wall admitted very little light. Cobwebs hung between the wooden beams that stretched above their heads, and Ben was sure that he could hear mice. It felt like the attic. If castles even had attics.

Since no one had come to meet them yet, Ben went over to the window and looked outside. He could see the incredible sweep of the valley below. There were still some splashes of sunlight, the sun setting behind the peaks. Snow had begun falling again.

"We were told that you would come," said a voice softly. Ben spun around, suddenly face to face with a girl who had emerged from the shadows.

"Mind you, we were expecting you slightly sooner."

"Who told you I was coming?" Ben needed to know.

"Burt, of course. She has great faith in you."

"Who's Burt?"

"Sorry, I meant Elizabeth," she said.

"Liza? Liza is still here, then?"

"Of course," she said, as Ben gave a big sigh of relief. "Where else would she be?"

"And she's all right?" he demanded.

"Well, she's locked up, but she's perfectly fine."

"Locked up here, like you are?" Whip asked.

"No, locked up downstairs," said the girl, some of the ease draining from her face.

"Downstairs?" *The one in the vault*, he remembered the woman saying. "Is that bad?"

"We need to get you inside. We can tell you everything then."

Chapter 27

SIBLING ARRIVALRY

The girl, whose name, she told them, was Sophia, led the way through a secret passageway, down into one of the locked dormitories. Ben regarded the passageway and then asked, "If you can get in and out, then why stay? Why not escape?"

"And go where? You saw the countryside. In this weather, it's perilous. They treat us okay in here as long as we behave."

Ben thought back to Mackenzie. How strange it was that both he and the girls shared the same predicament.

"Besides, Burt assured us we would be rescued. All we had to do was sit tight and wait."

"She means Elizabeth – Liza," another girl added, in case Ben had forgotten.

"We call her Burt," explained Sophia. "It's the nickname we gave her when she got here in September."

"Why do you call her Burt?"

"We all have nicknames like that. It's so the nuns don't know who we're talking about. Mine is Gus," Sophia said.

"Recently though, she has been called Black Burt because of what she did," said yet another girl, very proudly.

"Once she was taken downstairs, she told us that if anything were to happen to her, her parents, the Bloomswells, not the Bashfords, would be able to help," Sophia said.

"Who are the Bashfords?" Ben asked.

"They were supposed to be *you*, her family," she explained. "You see, on the first day of school, Burt was introduced to us as Beth *Bashford*. She only told us her real last name when she was locked up downstairs, and only after she made us all swear not to tell any of the nuns."

"What did Liza do?"

Some of the girls giggled.

"She fought back. Well, she tried to, but she was outnumbered. I never knew anyone who could do what she did with a frying pan." The girls continued to giggle quietly, exchanging looks of approval.

"Fought back against what, exactly? Tinmen?" Whip asked.

"Well, them too, but she fought the others, mostly."

"What others?"

"The people. The scientists, I guess. That's what she

thought they were. Burt kept going on about an experiment."

"Scientists? Experiments? What's going on here? And where are all the teachers? Where are all the other nuns?"

"That's just it, we don't know. They all disappeared, one by one, in the middle of the night. We'd wake up one morning and find another class without a teacher. A handful of them did eventually return, but they weren't the same as before."

"What do you mean?" asked Ben.

"They were *meaner*," answered another girl. "They had always been strict, but never mean about it."

"Yes, they weren't very nice after they came back. Oh! And then one night, we found Sister Francesca dead on the stairs."

"What? Really?" Ben asked.

"She was simply lying there, halfway up the stairs, her skin this awful color. It gives me goose bumps just to think of it," added another girl.

"How did she die?"

"We don't know, no one would tell us. They all acted as if it never happened."

"Sister Francesca was the first one to disappear and one of the few to come back," explained Sophia. "But it was when another sister also died that everyone except for Sister Rebecca disappeared again."

"Well, Sister Rebecca never disappeared in the first place. She was just mean from the beginning."

"We haven't seen the others since."

"And how did Liza get involved?" Ben asked.

"She was suspicious ever since Sister Francesca first disappeared and came back. Then, when she died, Burt became even more suspicious. She was the one who followed the body as it was taken downstairs. She apparently discovered something in one of the vaults. But that's all we know. She said the less we knew, the better. She'd intended to send your parents information about what was going on when she was caught in Our Mother's office and was locked up."

"But she's safe?"

"Oh, yes. We're under instructions to take you to her as soon as you get here."

Ben was soon following Sophia and one of the other girls down another secret passageway. He was trying to put answers to some of the questions he had. Barlow had implied that Liza had not been found yet. Was it possible that both Mr. Purchase and The Buyer had no idea that Liza had been here the entire time? Could a mere change of name have been responsible for Liza's safekeeping? Had they spent all of their time looking for Elizabeth Bloomswell and not Beth Bashford? Granted she had been locked up, but that was as punishment for being troublesome, not for being a Bloomswell!

"Careful with that step there," warned the girl behind him. "It's smaller than the rest. I've often tripped."

"Oh. Thank you."

The girl was about Ben's age, with a thick braid of red hair and a face full of freckles. She smiled broadly every time Ben happened to look her way.

"How do you know about this, these passageways?" Ben asked, just to break the silence.

"Well, it's our school. It's our home. Things get passed on you know, secrets, things students discover. We know everything about this place. It's how we sneak into the kitchens, or get outside whenever we like."

Ben thought again of Mackenzie and wondered if that was how he had discovered all the intricacies of Sugarhill.

"I'm Charlotte, by the way," said the redheaded girl. "But my nickname is Charlie; it's one of the easy ones. We really are so glad you've come."

"Thanks," said Ben, smiling. "We once had a dog named Charlie," he added, and instantly regretted it.

"That's nice," said Charlotte.

"We're almost there," said Sophia.

Liza was curled up fast asleep on her little strip of a bed when they crept into the vault.

Ben's heart was beating so fast that he wondered if he would be able to speak.

"Burt?" Sophia whispered, but there was no response.

Then Ben walked up to the bars and said her name. "Lizzie? Liza?"

At the sound of the familiar voice her eyes shot open, and she sat bolt upright. She spun around and squinted. She slowly climbed off her bed and inched closer, hardly believing what she was seeing.

"Liza?" Ben's voice was soft.

"Ben? Ben, is that you?"

"I've come to take you home, Liza," Ben said, and pushed his face between the bars.

Liza gasped, her eyes suddenly wet with tears, and she rushed forward, pushed her hands through the bars and pulled Ben in close.

"I thought, I thought..." she gasped. Ben's face was being squeezed against the bars, but he didn't care. "I thought I would never, no, but I did! I knew! I knew!" she said, fighting her tears.

She suddenly pushed him away from her, angry. "You carrot!" she snapped. "What took you so long? Do you know how long I've been in here, waiting?" she demanded.

"I am sorry! I am so sorry!" pleaded Ben.

A smile flashed across her face, followed by a scowl. "Well, don't do it again!" And then her great big smile reappeared. "What are you dressed as? And what did you do to your hair?"

"It's a long story. I'll tell you later."

"Are Mum and Dad upstairs?"

"Mum and Dad aren't here, Liz," answered Ben, a little wearily.

"What? Where are they?"

"I don't know."

Liza's smile went a little off kilter. "What do you mean, you don't know?"

"I mean I don't know. The last I saw of them was more

than three weeks ago, when they left me at Uncle Lucas's house."

"What were you doing there? Uncle Lucas is in America right now," she said.

"Not his house in London, his house in America!"

She looked at him in shock. "America? What were you doing in America?"

"Mum and Dad took me there!"

"Why would Mum and Dad take you to America? What about school?"

"I don't know! The fact is, they did! And I would love to ask them why, but they've disappeared!"

"Mum and Dad have disappeared?" she gasped.

"You don't know? It was in the newspapers and everything!"

"Well, pardon me for not keeping up with *The Evening Standard*, Ben! It's been a little difficult, what with being locked up in a stone vault!"

"The truth is, the newspapers sort of said that Mum and Dad were, well, sort of…"

"Sort of what?"

"Sort of dead."

"Dead?"

Ben nodded.

"They can't be!"

"Well, they're not! It's all very confusing, but we're assuming the article was fake. Well, not fake because two people did actually die, so that part's real, but fake in that it wasn't Mum and Dad."

"How do you know?"

"Because the dates the newspaper mentioned were all wrong. They were still with me when they were supposed to have been dead already. But no one knows where Mum and Dad are, and like I said, it's been almost a month since they've disappeared. The last *official* news was that they were dead, and there was a funeral and everything."

"Surely they can't just have disappeared! Whoever made the assumption that they're dead is an idiot. Olivander must know where they are! Why didn't you ask him?"

"It was a little difficult," he began, mimicking Liza, "what with being abandoned in an American orphanage and then left to die in a box! It wasn't like he was around to ask! Besides, he's gone missing, too!"

"Olivander isn't here either?" Liza's eyes were huge.

"No. I haven't seen him since I left England with Mum and Dad."

There was a long silence while Liza digested what Ben had told her.

"Then how did you get all the way here by yourself?" she asked finally.

"Well, I had help," Ben said, looking at Whip, who had already started to pick the lock to Liza's cell. "This is Whip."

"It's a pleasure to meet you. Ben here has told me so much about you," Whip said.

Liza smiled politely, but it was obvious she was confused. "How do you do? Wait, Ben, are you telling me that you traveled here all the way from Uncle Lucas's by yourself? What about Uncle Lucas? Couldn't he help?"

This was where Ben's optimism ended and cold, hard, fact took over. Mackenzie's words replayed in his head. *If he told you your uncle is dead, then your uncle is dead.*

"I'm afraid Uncle Lucas is dead, Lizzie."

Liza's face fell. "He's dead? How? When?"

"Back in New York, right when all of this started."

"How? How did he die?"

"They didn't say."

"They?"

"The people who killed him. The people who kidnapped me and left me for dead. The people who followed me back to England and then blew up the train I was on," Ben explained. "They're the same people that have been here at the school, Liza. Well, not the exact same people of course, but they all work for the same man. The man Mum and Dad have gone after." As soon as he said this, Ben realized there was still so much to tell Liza.

The two girls and Whip stood watch as Ben told Liza the whole story. He told her about the surprise visit to Uncle Lucas's house his parents had organized, about the roundabout journey via Bourgogne and the brief time spent with Uncle Lucas before seeing that fateful newspaper article. He told her about Sugarhill, Mackenzie and everything that led up to arriving at the harbor. He talked about meeting Mr. Holiday and Whip, their time on the ship, and the rest of the troupe. And after telling her about their journey from England to Heimweh, Ben finally told her about The Buyer. He was thoroughly exhausted once he had finished, and he wished he could just go to his room, close the door and sleep for a thousand years.

Liza took his hand and said, "I'm sure Mum and Dad are fine."

"I know," he said softly.

"But we won't be any good to them just sitting here and moping," she said, with a determined air. "We're Bloomswells. We fight back. Right?"

"Right," Ben said, a smile returning to his face.

"Okay, so now what? What's your plan?" Liza asked.

"Well, I didn't really think past this point, to be honest," Ben said.

"What? You don't have a plan to get us out of here?"

"No, we do," answered Whip. "We had an escort all set for tomorrow morning, but since we found you so quickly, we might as well get out of here tonight."

"But how will we get out? We can't really use the same way we got in," Ben said.

"How did you get in?" Liza asked.

"The coal delivery. A friend of Mr. Holiday helped us."

"Is that why you're so dirty?"

"Getting out isn't a problem," said Charlie. "We have a way that takes you right past the school walls, don't we?"

Sophia nodded.

"Like I said, getting out isn't the problem. It's having someplace to go."

"Yes, where will you be taking all of us?" Liza asked.

"Back to London, of course."

"And the girls?"

"The girls?" Ben and Whip chorused.

"Well, I can't just leave them all here, now can I?" Liza was suddenly indignant.

Ben looked to Whip for help, but he shrugged his shoulders awkwardly. They hadn't even thought of the other girls. And both of them knew that getting one girl out of the school was going to be a lot easier than getting all of them out.

"I just came for you, Liza. You're my sister. How would we get them all out without being discovered? Besides, where could we take them? And have you looked outside lately? It's not pretty, Liza."

"I'm not leaving them."

"Liz!"

"No!"

"Liz."

"I said, no!"

"Look, Elizabeth, I'm sorry, but right now we're the only ones who can help Mum and Dad – we're the only ones that know *to* help Mum and Dad! If we don't, no one else will."

"There must be some other way."

"Liz, Mum and Dad sacrificed themselves *and* you and me to do this. Surely whatever this is must be very important for them to do that. And I know it's tough, but surely you could make a sacrifice for the same purpose, because if you don't, someone else down the line is going to have to make an even bigger sacrifice, and then this decision won't even matter."

"Your brother's right, Burt," said Sophia. "Where will we go? All the way to England with you? How would we get there?"

"They should have thought of that," Liza said, annoyed.

"Your parents might not have come, but your brother and his friend are here. The three of you can go and get help. Find your parents and tell them exactly what's been going on."

"I couldn't possibly leave you all here!"

"We'll be all right. Besides, we've been waiting this long, I'm sure we can manage for a little while longer."

"But they're bound to notice that I'm not here. They'll know something is wrong."

"Someone will come and take your place. We'll take turns. As long as those metal men see that someone's in here, they're hardly likely to suspect anything. It should give you some time. We'll be fine, honestly. Go, get help. Get all of us home for Christmas."

Liza looked between the two girls and her brother, torn. "It's difficult, isn't it?" she said.

The girls hugged her. Liza nodded her head. "Shall I go and say goodbye to the girls?"

"I think the sooner we leave, the better. If you can show us that passage, we might even be able to get a train back to Zurich tonight, if we're lucky," Whip broke in.

"We can't leave yet though," Liza said.

"Why not?" demanded Ben.

"We have to get proof."

"Proof of what?"

"Proof of what's been going on here, Ben. Proof of *The Monarch Project.*"

"*The Monarch Project*? What's that?"

"It's the reason I tried to send word to Mum and Dad in the first place. I think these people are trying to kill the king!"

"Which king?"

"Our king, you carrot! It's the reason those people took over the school. St. Catharine's is involved somehow, something about certain minerals in the water up here in the mountains or something that they needed for the experiment to work; the one they were working on in the vaults. The experiment was what made the nuns change, and I'm sure it's what killed Sister Francesca and the others. I think it's how they're going to try to kill the king. And not only that, but when he's dead they intend to somehow sell the British throne. I don't know how, but I heard Sister Rebecca talking about a 'purchase' or something."

"It's all making sense now! This must be what Mum and Dad are trying to uncover!"

Ben and Whip looked at each other in shock.

"The Buyer wants the throne," Ben said.

"So you see, we must get proof so we can help Mum and Dad!" Liza said.

"What's the proof?" Ben asked.

"Papers I saw, blueprints and experiment graphs and things. They'll all be in Our Mother's office, I'm sure."

"Our Mother?" asked Ben.

"The Mother Superior."

"And where's that?"

"The second floor."

Chapter 28

A FLURRY OF SPLINTERS
AND SNOW

Sophia and Charlie were sent back upstairs with an update
for the other girls and goodbye messages from Liza. Liza in
turn took Ben and Whip to the Mother Superior's office,
lurking around corners and in the shadows with a keen eye
and ear for approaching danger.

"What about that woman?" Ben asked. "Is she alone? And
what about the tinmen?"

"Apart from the two groundsmen outside, there are only
two people here right now. Most everyone left when they
moved the equipment out of the vaults. The ones that stayed
behind are usually busy downstairs by now, and the tinmen
usually stay down with them," Liza told them.

The door to the Mother Superior's office had been left slightly ajar, enabling them to see that the room was empty. Liza immediately headed for the desk and rummaged through the papers that had been left lying on top. She also went through the drawers, pulling out random pieces of paper as she went along.

"See, look here," she said, showing them what she had found. "Sketches and layouts for those contraptions they had downstairs."

"What contraptions?" Ben asked.

"I'll have to tell you later," she said, stuffing papers into her satchel.

"What's this?" asked Ben, noticing a slip of paper that had fallen to the floor.

"Looks like a telegram," said Liza, reading over his shoulder. "A Mr. Barlow is to be expected here with more tinmen. Doesn't say when though."

Ben looked at Whip. So that's what Barlow was doing on the train – he was coming straight to St. Catharine's, and those tinmen were meant to come with him. The explosion was just to try and stop Ben, should they find him first.

"Well, that's not happening," Ben said. At least something good had come from what happened to Mr. Holiday.

Liza gave the desk one last look. "I think I have enough." With the sketches, letters and prints packed safely away in her satchel and underneath her jacket, Liza stepped out from behind the desk.

"What do we have here?"

Ben, Whip and Liza turned to face the door. The woman they had seen in the kitchen, together with another man and a group of tinmen, stood in the doorway.

"Sister Rebecca!" gasped Liza.

Whip readied his baseball bat, but the man in the doorway pulled out a pistol, aiming it at them. Ben recognized him as the other man who had taken him to Sugarhill.

"Coming back to the scene of the crime, are we?" Sister Rebecca said, taking a step forward. "And who are your friends, Miss Bashford? They're certainly not students here, are they?"

Cletus leaned closer to her and whispered. Her face froze.

"My goodness, you're the Bloomswell boy. You're supposed to be dead. What are you doing here?" she asked, stupefied. She looked at Liza for an answer, but then Ben could see by her changing expression that she'd come up with it all by herself.

"Elizabeth Bloomswell," she said darkly, a malevolent smile slithering across her face. "Weren't you clever?" She seemed genuinely impressed with Liza. "You were here the entire time, and no one was ever the wiser because of your little name change. What will he say when I tell him I have both the Bloomswell children?"

Liza stepped in front of Ben, and Whip repositioned his bat, ready to strike. Sister Rebecca grimaced and put her hand up.

"I am sorry to have to ruin what I'm sure was going to be such a happy reunion," she said, "but we really only need one of you. Get me the boy," she instructed a tinman.

"The boy," she said again, and the tinman stepped forward.

"Wait! Take me instead, I beg you!" cried Liza.

"Liza, no!" Ben yelled.

Sister Rebecca again put up her hand. The tinman stopped in his tracks.

"Just think! You'd be the one to give him Ben! And he would be alive, thanks to you! Surely that would mean something? And besides, how are you going to explain the fact that while everyone was combing half the western world for Ben, I was right here under your very nose?"

Liza had hit a nerve.

Sister Rebecca flinched ever so slightly and said, "My gracious, Elizabeth! What a grand gesture. It's not like you to get so emotional. Who would have thought?" She considered the proposal for a moment. She would be reprimanded for not having realized that Elizabeth Bloomswell was within her grasp the whole time, and it scared her. "Very well," she said.

"I want to say something to my brother first," Liza said. She turned to Ben and hugged him, putting her mouth close to his ear.

"I've got a plan," she whispered. "Do you see that painting of the old man, on your right?" Ben glanced at it quickly. "Jump through it and run. There's a passageway behind it. Follow it downstairs, and we will meet you there." She pulled herself away from him and looked him in the eye. "I love you."

Then she turned and faced the group. "I'm ready."

"Oh, my dear," said Sister Rebecca. "You have no idea what to be ready for."

Liza stuck out her hands as if waiting to be handcuffed, and the tinman came forward. He was about to take hold of her wrists when Liza suddenly shouted, "Now!"

Ben made a dash for the painting.

Whip leapt forward as the pistol went off, the bullet burying itself in the back wall. He swung his baseball bat, severing the tinman's head and sending it flying into Cletus before he could take another shot.

Sister Rebecca lunged at Liza, her hands like talons. Liza jerked to the left, spinning around and bringing both her elbows down onto Sister Rebecca's back. Then, in one continuous movement, she reached out and took hold of two canes in the umbrella stand. She brandished them like swords, making it impossible for any of them to follow Ben as he ripped through the lacquered canvas.

He so badly wanted to help, to stay and fight, but he was determined to do as Liza had asked. He ran down the little spiral staircase, and all he could hear were thuds and thumps as canes and baseball bat met tin.

Because it was dark, he did not see the door in front of him and ran straight into it, full force, bashing it open. When he regained his bearings he saw that the main staircase was right in front of him, and a mere floor below were the main doors to the school. All he had to do was get to the dormitories. He was about to run for it when he heard the gunshot.

Silence fell. His blood froze.

Then he heard another thud, followed by the bright crack of wood. Terrified that Liza had been hurt, Ben raced up the main stairs to see what had happened. But Liza was coming down the stairs, and she seemed perfectly fine, if not more than a little angry. She was helping Whip walk by supporting his weight, his right arm around her shoulders. Ben saw that he was bleeding from his torso. Cletus's final, frenzied shot must have hit him. Liza was still holding onto the handle of one cane, the only part left after she cracked it over Cletus's head.

"We're leaving!" she shouted, grabbing Ben's arm and pulling him to Whip's other side to help.

"Where's the passage?" Ben asked.

"Why bother? They know we're leaving. Let's just go through the main doors!" They raced down the stairs as fast as they could, and they were halfway to the main doors when Ben heard the sounds of tin feet on stone.

"Hurry!" shouted Liza.

The dark figure heard the unmistakable crack of a gunshot from deep within the school, and pushed himself even harder through the falling snow. If anything had befallen his target, his revenge would be relentless. A gunshot wound, or even death, would cower in comparison to what he would do to those guilty.

He made quick work of clambering over the gate and sprinted towards the massive main doors of St. Catharine's.

Ben, Liza and Whip were only able to take a few more steps toward the doors before the banging started. Something big or strong, or probably both, was trying to get inside by ramming against the main doors. Whatever it was, it didn't sound friendly.

They pulled back and looked around for another means of escape. Ben thought they should try the secret passage after all, but tinmen had come to block all of the exits, trapping them.

"Where are they all coming from?" Liza gasped.

Bang! Bang! Bang! sounded at the door. Sister Rebecca had made her way to the banister.

"Bring them to me," she ordered.

As one, the tinmen stepped forward.

Behind them, the doors cracked loudly. The three of them turned to face the door as another *bang* reverberated through the hall, and they watched in terror as the door finally broke off its hinges. In the roar and the flurry of splinters and snow that blew in, they could just see a dark figure. They stepped back instinctively, fearful and unsure. As the figure stepped completely into the light, realization dawned, and Ben shivered with goose bumps.

"Olivander!" he burst out.

Whip stared in disbelief. His mouth slowly dropped open. Was the pain causing this hallucination, or was he really looking at a man made of wood? Could the light be playing tricks? No. He could see the faint twists and turns of the grain, the wrinkles all over the chiseled face. He could see the carved fingers and details of the knuckles, the forearms like baseball bats. He could see it all, and all he could say was, "Oh, my."

The second Olivander saw Ben and Liza, the annoyance that he had carried with him for the past few weeks was replaced by a mixture of euphoria and gratitude. He'd finally found his young masters! He'd finally been able to comply with the task given him by their parents – his employers – the task of protecting their children.

This new feeling was almost instantly replaced by another feeling – absolute rage that somebody had dared threaten his wards. He could see from both the children's faces, and the state of the stranger they were helping, that he had arrived in the nick of time. He resolved not to waste any more of it.

The wooden man's sudden intrusion didn't seem to have any effect on the approaching tinmen. They continued drawing closer. One tinman especially was getting too close to the children, and consequently triggered Olivander's retaliation.

Olivander doubled over, putting his hands on the floor to use them as a pushing-off point as he hopped backwards up against the door frame. Then, like a massive jack-in-the-box, he hurtled forwards again, using his legs as a spring mechanism to propel himself. He was nothing more than a blur as he shot through the air and into the nearest tinman.

He pulled it down effortlessly, smashing its head against the floor to flatten it. He seemed to take particular enjoyment in stepping on the squashed head with the heel of his boot.

The other tinmen surrounded him and started their attack.

Nothing seemed to hurt or deter Olivander. His arms whipped around. Punches were thrown. Hits were blocked. Tinmen heads were punched through and *insignias* pulled off, rendering the tinmen completely still.

There was a din of clanging metal as Olivander fought. To Ben, it sounded as if a cook was throwing a tantrum in the kitchen.

Whip stared in amazement. "What is he exactly? What is he made of?" he asked.

"Wood," Liza confirmed. "But no one knows what kind. No one's ever been able to find out, and he won't say," she said, with a gleam in her eyes.

"I told you he would come in handy!" Ben shouted.

Olivander stood in the middle of the ring of debris, the hall finally silent. He looked up at the landing to see if the woman had anything else for him, but there was no one there. Sister Rebecca was gone. He stepped over the rubble and walked towards Ben, Liza and their companion, his wooden limbs moving smoothly underneath his leather suit.

He didn't even have time to stop and crouch down before Ben rushed towards him and hugged him. He put his hand on Ben's head.

"I knew you'd find us," Ben said quietly.

"Hello, 'Vander," Liza said, and she smiled broadly.

Whip was still staring. He studied the fine workmanship that had gone into carving Olivander's face. He was especially amazed by the intricacy of his motionless eyes, which seemed to follow you around the room. When he was introduced to Olivander all he could say was, "Incredible."

Are you all right? Olivander asked in sign language.

"Yes, we're fine," Liza answered. "Whip needs some help though."

I'll see to him, signed Olivander, easing him off Liza's shoulders. He helped Whip to the floor and made quick work of tending to his injury.

It is a clean wound, he signed.

"He says it's a clean wound," Liza began to translate, but Whip interrupted her. "It's okay, I understand him."

Olivander continued, *The bullet passed straight through. Aside from the pain in his side, it should cause no further trouble.*

Whip was surprised at how gentle Olivander was, when moments before he had been almost savage. He even found some comfort in the cool touch of the wooden hands as they deftly dressed his wound.

Ben, in the meantime, kept a watchful eye on the slain tinmen, ready to fight back in case any of them managed to get back up. None of them so much as stirred. He could not help but be impressed by Olivander, too.

"Where did Sister Rebecca go?" asked Liza, coming up behind him.

"Don't know," Ben replied. "She probably ran away."

"Only if she knows what's good for her," Liza said. "I'm going to check on the girls, just to make sure she hasn't gone up there."

It's not safe for you to go on your own, we can't...

" 'Vander, I'll be fine. Trust me. I have to go check on the girls."

Olivander looked at her for a moment, then nodded his head.

"Here, take the bat, just in case," Whip offered. "It looks like you're good at hitting things, too."

Tell them they won't have to wait much longer. Tell them help is on the way, tonight even.

"Tonight?" Liza asked.

Yes. So, hurry. We cannot be seen here. We will be detained, and we must hurry.

Liza ran off, and Olivander returned his attention to Whip. Ben crouched down across from Olivander and smiled at him.

"Mum and Dad not with you, are they? Not perhaps still waiting outside for a dramatic entrance?"

Olivander shook his head.

Ben sighed. He had kept his eyes trained on the doorway as Olivander fought, hoping, half-expecting to see his parents charge in after him.

"I knew you'd find us. I just knew it!" he said again.

Olivander lifted his face to Ben's.

"How did you know we were here? I mean, I guess you could..." The many things that could have led Olivander to St. Catharine's ran through his head, but the answer suddenly became very obvious, making Ben feel a little silly. "Oh, you knew Liza was here. I mean, you probably just came for her."

I followed you, Olivander signed, keeping his hand extended on the word "you," as if to accentuate it. *Liza was safe for the time being. You were who I needed to protect. You were what was important above all else. I am sorry I could not get to you sooner. I will not fail you again.*

"You didn't fail me. Don't be daft."

I thought I had lost you forever at Sugarhill.

"Sugarhill? How do you know about Sugarhill?"

I was there.

"But how did you know I was there?"

I followed you.

"But how? How did you know?"

The key your mother gave you.

Ben suddenly remembered the key to No. 4. He pulled it

out from underneath his jacket, and looked at it, confused. "What about it?"

Olivander pointed to the small wooden fob attached to the key loop. *I followed me. A part of me has always been with you.*

Ben held the fob between his thumb and forefinger and inspected it closely. "This is a part of you?"

It once was.

Ben could not stop his jaw from dropping. What he held in his hand was suddenly a whole lot more than just a key fob.

"Where did you take it from? Where on your body?" He needed to know.

Olivander pointed to the back of his neck, and Ben got up to look. There, at the back of his neck, were four, small, rectangular holes, one above the other. He matched the fob with a hole, and it fit perfectly.

"Did it hurt?"

Olivander shook his head.

"There are four of them."

One for each of you.

"Each of us? So Mum and Dad each have one, too?"

He nodded.

"So do you know where they are?"

Olivander shook his head.

"But…"

I lost them when I came to look for you. The distance between us grew too great, and I could no longer feel them.

"Oh." Ben could feel his heart grow heavy.

That's why I had to hurry to get to you. I did not want to lose you as well. But I will retrace my steps and find them again, no matter how long it takes. I will find out where they are.

"Cairo," Ben said casually, almost like he was telling someone what day of the week it was. And as soon as he realized what he had said, he remembered the folded up telegram.

"Cairo! *Cairo!*" he shouted, as he searched his clothes. "Father's in Cairo!"

How do you know?

"Because of this!" he said, finally pulling out the folded piece of paper. "A man named Farden found Father and says he's in Cairo!"

Olivander unfolded the telegram and inspected it. "You can believe Farden," Whip said. "If he says he's in Cairo, the man's in Cairo," he told Olivander, with a knowing smile to Ben.

Olivander inspected the wrinkled telegram a moment longer, then signed, *Then we must go to Cairo.*

Ben couldn't help but shout out in excitement.

"What's going on?" asked Liza, as she ran back, hearing the commotion.

"Father's in Cairo, and we're going to go get him!"

"Cairo? *Really?*"

It appears so.

"Is Mum with him?" Liza asked.

I don't know, he answered.

Liza looked at Ben, who also shook his head. There was an uncomfortable moment of silence.

"Too bad she can't simply pick up the phone and call for help like you did," Ben said, putting his arm under Whip's to help him stand.

"Right," Liza said, but then what Ben had said struck her. "Wait, what?"

"I said, too bad Mum can't pick up the phone."

"No, I heard you, but what are you talking about? I never called you."

"Well, all right, you might've intended to call Uncle Lucas, but I answered the phone. You said, 'Tell Mr. Bashford his niece is in danger.'"

"Ben, I never called anyone! How could I call you from here? I mean, look at the place! We don't even have electricity, much less a telephone."

Ben had goose bumps again.

"You mean..." Ben began.

"It must've been Mum! I mean, who else could it have been? No one else knows I'm here!"

"That makes sense, doesn't it?" Ben asked.

"It makes perfect sense! And at least it means we know she was okay then. Maybe Dad knows where she is. Perhaps she's even with Dad! Right?" she asked Olivander.

It is very possible.

"Well, then, let's go!" the children chorused.

First we must get to safety and devise a plan. Are the others all right?

Liza took a deep breath. "They heard the commotion, but Sister Rebecca never went up there. There are some things missing from Our Mother's office, so I reckon she made a run for it. The girls are fine. They said to say thank you."

Then we must go, Olivander said, and put his arm under Whip's to help him stand.

Ben looked from his sister to Olivander, and was suddenly aware of feeling quite different. Something had shifted, something had changed. And unlike when it happened before, it was making him feel good. And he realized, almost by surprise, that he had done it. What he had set out to do more than three weeks ago had been accomplished. He had found his sister. He had even gained back their trusted friend. His quest was over.

But as he looked between them again, he knew that all of it, from escaping from Sugarhill, to trekking back to the city, to narrowly eluding Barlow on the pier, all of it was just the start of it. There was much, much more to do. Nothing was over. And maybe it was just the sudden feeling of success, and being there among them, but the thought of more to come excited him.

"This is just the beginning, isn't it? We've a lot more to do, haven't we?" he asked Olivander.

Yes, Olivander nodded.

"Mum and Dad are still out there, and they need our help."

"So, then," Liza said, "let's not waste any more time."

Ben took a deep breath and looked at Whip. "Are you okay to move?"

"It's only a flesh wound. I'm all set."

Ben looked at Liza, who smiled encouragingly at him. "Let's go find Mum and Dad," he said.

Then, with a nod to Olivander, he led the way, as the four of them walked out of St. Catharine's and into the snow.

Acknowledgements

To Jana Loughlin, whom without, without a doubt, none of this would have happened; who always listened, no matter how many rewrites or ideas; knew what I meant to say and helped me say it; and who shared my excitement from the beginning. For that, and so much more, thank you.

To Adrienne Kress and her Ironic Gentleman, who lead the way and showed me what was possible; who remains so generous with her knowledge, wisdom and know-how; and for being instrumental in Ben becoming a boy.

To Kira Lynn, who saw it for what it could be, and helped me prune it to what it has become.

And finally, to the ladies of The Gilford Public Library of New Hampshire (2007-2008) who generously catered to my every research whim and made me feel like a real writer.

To you all, a great deal of thanks and gratitude.